UNEXPECTED CAPTAIN

LAYLA STONE

PROMPT PENWORK

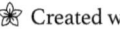

CONTENTS

1

INNOCENT

The meeting had ended, and everyone was now retreating from Captain Rannn's office. It had been weeks since the battle with Fynbar and his killer bots. They'd won, but all this time had been spent locating the slaves and healing them as best as Ansel could.

Chollar and his new mate were slow to exit the office. Rannn assumed the telepath had something to say, maybe a warning regarding what someone had been thinking. Rannn didn't care.

He couldn't care. Mostly because he couldn't concentrate on anything but the images in his head. Good Seth, he was thankful that no one had noticed how truly lost he felt.

The mission was over, they were headed back to Garna, and he had his own issues to worry about. Namely, whether or not he was still fit to be captain. The vast horrors he'd experienced courtesy of the memories he had gained, knowledge of the crime the sadistic Numan had committed for hundreds of years, tortured him.

The things that Fynbar had done. They horrified and consumed him so much that he didn't even remember if he had showered today or not.

Even now, he flashed on a memory of Fynbar cutting out a male's rib cage and installing organs of his own design. The male had bled out within hours. The cybernetic organs were not aligned right when installed. An entire life gone because of a miscalculation.

Another memory from Fynbar slithered across Rannn's mind. The time he'd unleashed nanites into a prison cell, infecting two families. The nanites had destroyed the part of the brain that controlled the feeling of being sated. Less than a week later, they started to eat each other. That was after they had eaten their clothes.

So much evil.

Rannn had to push those thoughts back. He had a ship to run, a crew to think about. Rannn had to get his crew back to safety. Back to Garna. Deep down, he felt as if his mind were crumbling, and he didn't know how long he would last.

Rannn gasped and hit a knee.

Searing, white-hot pain clawed into his mind. He had no idea why. He hadn't done anything, had he?

His whole body shook. Grabbing his head, Rannn couldn't see anymore, and he wasn't sure if he had closed his eyes or if the pain had blinded him.

All he could do was survive the burn. Images of death and carnage flashed quickly behind his eyes. Blood, death, bodies, cries, pleas...it was too much.

Rannn could smell the floor and feel the hardness of it as he pushed his forehead against the coolness. Faint groans echoed in his ears. His heart pumped hard in his chest as he kept gasping for breath.

Was he dying? What was happening?

The mental claws receded, and he felt his body being lifted into the air. Floating weightlessly. It took a few extra seconds to open his eyes.

He could breathe easier. His chest was...his whole body no longer felt constricted.

When he felt his feet, Rannn leaned over and grabbed the table, taking a deep breath. It was all he could do, considering that his brain felt like it had been beaten and scrambled. But it didn't take more than a millisecond to figure out what had happened.

Chollar had removed the evil Numan's memories.

Gone.

Rannn couldn't recall anything. And he tried.

Rannn hadn't known that Chollar could do that. If he had, he would have asked him to do it seconds after he'd gotten back. Even though his head felt fatigued, and he was still recovering from the onslaught, Rannn tried to voice his genuine gratitude.

His voice was lost, though. His brain lagging.

Chollar didn't bother waiting for a thank you. Instead, the Master Elder Cerebral said, "And just so you know, Nue didn't lie to you. She didn't change or forge her prison transfer paperwork. And the reason she was being sent to Debsa is because the Federation messed up and thinks she's a contract killer named Nova."

Rannn was dead-silent. He understood the words but couldn't process them.

"Also, you're right to assume she's going to try and escape the ship the second you get back. Considering how you locked her down, you've fed her fear. She thinks the second you go back, you are sending her to Debsa. So, either stop being a coward and do what you really want to do, or let her escape."

Rannn watched Chollar leave the room, hand-in-hand with his mate. The warning echoed through his mind. *Nue didn't lie to you.* It was a crushing blow to his soul.

He remembered being furious when he found out.

Irate that another female had lied to him so convincingly.

And to think, she'd thought his anger would force him to send her to a prison planet that would take her life.

Slumping into the nearest chair, Rannn leaned back, closed his eyes, and cursed. By all the power of Seth, he had become his worst nightmare. He had become his father, unable to see past his duty. His responsibilities. Unwilling to see the truth in a female's eyes.

Rannn remembered the look in his sister's eyes when she told him about what had happened to her. Rannn had vowed to himself right then never be so heartless.

Seth of Stars, he couldn't breathe.

He'd failed.

2

YUNKIN JERKS

No one talked to her.

No one even looked at her.

Considering how long she had been imprisoned in Rannn's cabin, she'd expected someone to at least say something. Was sympathy too much for these people? Or was their silence something His Highness—the captain—required, forbidding everyone from even breathing in her direction?

The jerk had probably told everyone that she'd escaped prison and was a cold-hearted murderer.

She hated him. Her blood burned at the sight of him.

Did no one else notice how off he was? Or did they just pretend they didn't see because he was the leader? Idiots.

Rannn was exactly like every other Yunkin she had met. Belittling, a rat bastard that refused to see that Yunkins weren't the honorable race they claimed to be—they were prejudiced cowards.

All claimed they were honor incarnate when they just... made up laws to fit their assumptions.

When Rannn was on the bridge with his crewmember Yon,

pretending that everything was right in their world, that Rannn was a hero because he saved a few hundred slaves.

Though it wasn't like he was Seth of Stars and did it all on his own.

The team had saved everyone, not just Rannn.

Rannn was not a good guy.

He was quick to give commands and expected instant obedience. As if he were a god. He was everything she hated. She couldn't wait until she got back into Federation space. With luck, she would be gone in less than an hour after reaching Garna.

Or at least, she hoped.

She couldn't take another second under this Yunkin's direction.

Forcing herself to get to work, Nue scanned the millions of lightyears of space, planning and projecting a flight path so the ship didn't end up colliding with a planet, a dark hole, or any of the hundreds of other things that would instantly kill them.

Sending her preliminary flight plan to Yon, she told him, "I can get you as far as the asteroid belt, but you will have to fly manually through it. Then you can pick up the flight path on the other side."

"Will do," said Yon as he initiated the engines and took off.

3

SENNITES

Rannn pushed himself off his seat, no longer willing to give in to his guilt. He had to find Nue and apologize. And then he had to spend every single minute from now until he reached Garna, clearing her record.

Because according to the Federation, she was guilty.

All the things he'd done and said to her ate him up inside, but his honor for the past few weeks demanded that he not let a prisoner go free. The charges against her had made her look like a soulless monster. And he'd told himself that her pitiful act was just that—an act.

Finding out that she was telling the truth made him feel like someone had kicked out his knees. Except his legs weren't throbbing in pain.

She is telling the truth.

Rannn could still hear Chollar's words. Hell, he could practically taste them.

The Minky screen pinged, drawing him from his dark thoughts. It was a video call

from Commander Vivra, the acting captain on his assigned star carrier.

Duty and responsibility washed over him, shoving down his feelings of guilt and remorse and making him focus on what was most important: his crew, his ship, and the next mission to find Calum.

Pressing the connect button, he spoke as Vivra's green face appeared on the screen. "Commander."

"Captain, there's a problem."

Inhaling slowly, he felt his shoulders roll back. "What's the problem?"

Vivra's green eyes peered over at Clalls, the Night Demon-Yunkin hybrid who stood next to her. With his pale white skin, chopped, spiky hair, and sharp, two-inch-long teeth, Clalls was the kind of Demon that stood out, even among his own kind.

Stepping into camera range, he said, "I've caught a handful of communication splices that were sent out from the Sennite planet. They've shut down all landing pads and stopped all space commerce."

"What are you saying, Clalls? Are you suggesting they are being hostile?"

"No," he said. "The bits I've recovered suggest they are experiencing a subnormal number of births."

Rannn didn't see the correlation. So, he simply waited for the Demon to explain further. When Clalls didn't say another word, Rannn held up his hands. "Okay. How many is a subnormal number?"

"Zero births over the past year. Doctors can't find a reason, and women are starting to call it an unknown disease."

"That's impossible. If there were a disease sweeping the planet for over a year, we would know about it."

Clalls tilted his head. "Are you questioning my information? Because I can assure you, the Sennites have had no births. And they are now starting to freak out. They've reached out to every high-ranking medical doctor for a cure, and no one can understand it. And they have been doing thousands of tests."

Damn arrogant Sennites had waited too long. They should have asked for help a year ago. Garna was the only ship equipped to handle planet-wide issues like this, and Rannn really didn't want to give up the resources. He wanted to look for Calum first.

Rannn dragged his hand over his head. "I'll have Ansel contact their Planet Health Organization and see if he can help."

Clalls lifted a white brow. "They've shut down all communication. Ansel won't be able to get through."

Rannn could see the Sennites doing something like that. They would keep their secrets close and figure out their own problems. But this was bigger than just them. If it was a disease and spread to other planets...

Facing forward, he told Vivra, "To be clear, the Federation has been alerted?"

"No."

To Clalls, he asked, "Did you obtain those slices legally?"

The Demon shrugged. "Sure."

Pointing at the screen, Rannn said, "Get documentation and then send it to the Sennite admiral with a note to call me." Checking his Minky watch, he did the math. He then added, "Tell her if she doesn't call me in two hours, I'll log the petition for a planet-wide quarantine and court-martial her for keeping it a secret and possibly infecting other planets."

Clalls smiled, showing his long, sharp teeth. It was his normal, pretentious smile. "I'd love to, Captain."

Rannn nodded as he terminated the call. Then he initiated a video call to Ansel. The Numan accepted after two rings.

"Captain." Ansel tilted his head. "Hmmm. You look better."

Rannn didn't have a response to that. Perhaps he hadn't been as convincing as he'd thought with looking like he was keeping it together. Clearing his throat, he said, "The Sennites are suffering from some kind of epidemic. No births from anyone in over a year. The entire planet. Do you think this is Calum's work?"

Ansel crossed his arms and leaned back slightly. "Considering it's planet-wide, I'd say yes. But Calum's mental degradation and corruption has shown that he prefers total extinction. With that, I'd say it was probably someone else. Do the numbers include non-Sennite females who live on the planet?"

"Not that Clalls told me. But I don't know."

"I need more data. I will call the planet physician and see what she says."

"Clalls said they closed all communications," Rannn said.

"My credentials should speak for themselves. They will want my help," Ansel said, looking away from the screen. "Is that where we're headed next?"

Of course, that was where they were headed next. "You know the answer to that."

"I have some preliminarily ideas that I need to think about. I'll talk to you later." Ansel said all of that while not once looking at Rannn. The captain terminated the call and mentally calculated how long it would be before he arrived back at Garna, and then how long it would take for the ship to arrive at Sennite.

Maybe it would be a good idea to have Vivra head there now. He could catch up. Liking that idea, he sent the order, and his gut eased.

Now it was time to find Nue and do what he must.

4

APOLOGY

Nue had yet to finalize the flight plan when she heard the captain walk in. She glanced back, and Rannn was headed straight for her.

Great.

Turning all the way around, she couldn't wait to hear what he had to say now. Another threat? A step-by-step plan for how he was going to escort her to Debsa?

"I need you to come with me."

To be locked in his cabin again?

No, thank you.

"I'm not finished. I need to get some semblance of an idea of what's in the asteroid belt. Yon can fly through it manually, but I should give him intel so we continue in the correct direction."

"Are we at the asteroid belt?"

"No." What was he getting at?

Rannn cut his eyes to the pilot. "Yon, leave the bridge."

Yon stood up immediately, grabbed his mate's hand, and walked out. Nue could feel her heart beating a little faster.

What the hell was going on?

"I wanted to privately apologize to you before I notified the crew of my error."

His error?

Nue wasn't an idiot. He couldn't possibly be talking about the error of her being a convicted felon.

"You are innocent of the murder charges, and I didn't believe you. I didn't trust you. I took the words in the file as law and didn't realize they had confused you with someone else. And for that...I'm sorry."

Was she dreaming? There was no way Rannn knew about Nova.

Nue had fantasized about this moment for a long time. Dreamed about Rannn's expression when he found out that she was innocent. To feel the validation she knew she was owed. But this was not playing out like her fantasy at all.

Nothing about this felt validating. Just a whole lot of *meh*.

"I will clear your record and add my personal account of your innocence. It should be done before we arrive on Garna." He looked away, and she saw his jaw tighten. "Since there is no record of how you came to be Federation, I can add you as a FAVII if you want to stay on as a part of the crew."

"Thank you," was all she could say. She was confused. Why was he offering her a place on the team? She was still a felon. She'd hacked the Federation maps and updated them—not a crime in her mind, but breaking into the Federation servers were not a good thing. Hence the criminal case and a flight to Debsa.

But he didn't seem to know about that.

"Are you thanking me for clearing your record, or allowing you to stay on as a part of the team?"

Really? "The first one."

He nodded tightly. "Just to be clear, after your record is clear, you *don't* want to stay on as a part of the crew?"

With him as her captain. No. She wasn't an idiot.

"No, I don't."

"Okay, then. I will make sure to have transportation waiting for you when we return." He cleared his throat and added, "You are entitled to write a letter to my commanding admiral with any grievances you have against my actions. I encourage you to write one. I know how I've acted towards you."

That knocked her out of her stupor. He knew how he'd treated her? Was that an apology? *Oh, I'm sorry I mistreated you. Write a grievance letter to my commanding officer, who will do nothing about it.*

Bastard.

What a Yunkin thing to do.

"Okay," was all she said.

"I will inform the crew through a ship-wide message that you are no longer a person of questionable character and that you are free to move around the ship unescorted."

That was decent of him. Almost honorable. But it was more like him covering his ass. And to be honest, his apology was dry and unfeeling.

As if he knew the words to say, but they didn't come from the heart. It didn't sound like he was really sorry. It sounded like he was trying to set things right—as Yunkins did—but it just felt hollow.

"How did you find out that I was innocent? Because I doubt you just came to your senses."

She didn't care if she offended with her words; she wanted answers. And she said them, hoping the telepath had heard her. Though considering all the things he *hadn't* told Rannn... The jerk.

Weeks of crap from Rannn, and not once did that male step in and defend her. Nue had assumed he would have at least come to talk to her about her thoughts. But he never did. And she never noticed anything odd in her mind.

As if the telepath didn't care to listen to her thoughts.

It was an odd emotional stance to have: not wanting to lose her privacy and yet expecting to be violated.

His eyes cut to her. "This was an apology. Not an opening for an interrogation."

Nue's mouthed opened. Did he really just snap at her for asking how he'd figured it out?

"I wasn't interrogating you. I was asking a question. I expected you would know the difference."

"I don't really care if you accept my apology. I want to make sure you understood that I am acknowledging my error and fixing it."

She just stared.

Yunkins.

He honestly thought he didn't have to be sincere. He just had to fix it. What. An. Idiot.

Returning her attention to the screen, she said, "I really don't care about your apology because it's meaningless. When and if you actually feel sorry for locking me in your cabin and not believing a word I said about not being a murderer, *then* you can come back and try again."

"By all means, hold your breath for that," he said dismissively.

By all that was holy, she wanted to stab him so badly.

Rolling her eyes, she said, "Don't you have walls to stare at? Or halls to mumble in by yourself?"

Rannn lifted his chin, and she saw how much what she'd said bothered him.

Good.

Without another word, he walked out. Nue felt a little smug

at getting the last word. He really was a jerk, and she didn't feel an ounce of remorse. "

Tapping the Minky screen, she went back to looking over the vast expanse of space, disregarding detection of some small motion. The objects wouldn't hit this pirate ship with its current trajectory. Moving to the next few million light years, she scanned the upcoming asteroid belt.

The door opened, and she instinctively turned, wondering if Rannn had come back to tell her that he hadn't meant what he said, and she was going to Debsa.

To her surprise, Sci, one of the ship's telepaths, walked in.

"Come to apologize, too? Took you long enough to tell Rannn the truth." Nue wasn't usually snappy, but she was still pissed.

"People can convince themselves of anything," Sci said calmly.

No, he spoke in the way an adult talked to a child who was throwing a tantrum. "Plenty of criminals think they did the right thing. Or that they had no other choice. I don't have the ability to search your memories and prove you didn't kill that male. All I heard was your constant hate for Rannn, and your belief that you didn't deserve to be incriminated."

Folding her arms, she sat, her posture stiff. "Then what changed your mind? Why make him believe I'm not a felon? Because when he finds out that I am, he's going to be pissed." And he might try to send her to Debsa again.

"I didn't. My brother did. He can search memories. And he saw the truth. Chollar told Rannn that you weren't the killer. That Nova was. But he is only going off your memories and not hard facts, so he could be wrong," Sci said in a way that irked her.

Nue hadn't killed anyone, and if he didn't believe her...she didn't give a damn.

Sci continued. "Chollar also told Rannn that you were going to jump ship. Which is what you want to do, but I am here to tell you to wait. The safest place is with the captain and his crew. Especially while a war is raging between us and Calum the disease maker. If you leave, you could die from whatever pestilence he unleashes. And he *will* unleash something."

Nue pulled her lips back, not liking the idea of staying on the ship. But she also knew about the crazy scientist, Calum. Sasha had told her about him when they first started this mission.

Sci took a deep breath. "I also want to say that I'm sorry for not reaching out to you and at least trying to verify if the charges were true or false. I discouraged myself because you have a tendency to dwell on Rannn's demise."

That wasn't fair. She was just reacting to Rannn's threats.

"No, Nue, it was not just a reaction. You cultivated those thoughts, you perpetuated them. You fed them," Sci said sternly, and she hated each and every word.

Slapping the Minky screen, she yelled, "He was going to take me to Debsa. The hellhole planet where I would have died because those Federation officers that run the place are corrupt. And I was just supposed to...what? Be okay with that?"

Sci was only silent for a moment before he said, "I find it interesting that you hate Rannn more than you hate your sister, who was the reason you were falsely accused of being a murderer. Wouldn't a true sister who cared about you have come forward and turned herself in?"

Those words turned to acid in Nue's stomach.

She was angry with her sister. But Nova had become a Rana, a special female group of contract assassins. So, whoever the guy was that Nova had killed, he'd probably deserved it. Hopefully. But Nova had also helped Nue escape Debsa before she was admitted. So, regardless of her ruined record. Nova still watched out for her.

"Rannn is not your enemy," Sci said.

"There is nothing you can say about Rannn that will make me think he is anything but a stubborn, arrogant, honor-twisted Yunkin," Nue said with fervent vehemence.

Sci's eyes narrowed. "You don't know anything about him. You don't understand the lengths he will go to, to protect his crew. To keep them safe."

"He didn't give one second's thought to my safety when he locked me in his cabin, unable to escape. If we had to abandon ship, I would have died while locked inside."

Sci's nostrils flared. "You don't know what you're talking about. There was no option to abandon ship."

She was about to argue when Sci held up his hand. "Stop. And just watch."

Immediately, images consumed her mind.

The bridge was gone, and she saw a fast-forward version of being attacked by little bots. Then the breach of the planet and the rescue of enslaved cyborgs.

It was bloody, and Rannn got hurt. His angry flared every time a cyborg slave died. He used his body to shield the sleeping cyborgs from the black bots.

Rannn carried slaves to the pickup zone over and over again without slowing down.

Nue watched Rannn take the lead when entering a new building. He made sure he was the first one in.

The images disappeared, and Nue's head hurt. Grabbing the console, she tried to push the images of Rannn being someone she didn't know out of her head.

The Rannn she'd just witnessed was not the same Yunkin she hated.

Conflicted, she almost told Sci that she understood why he

respected Rannn so much. But it would denote that she didn't. Conflict now warred inside her. After seeing that...she admired Rannn's unwavering dedication to everyone's safety.

On that planet, he had been a leader. But the jerk who'd talked to her just a minute ago, *he* was something else.

Behind her, the navigation dash buzzed. Turning, she opened the visual screen and saw a rogue comet spinning directly toward them.

"What the hell?" Nothing should have been yanked into their gravitational pull.

Yon and Rannn rushed through the door to the bridge, and she immediately called out the direction from which the mass was coming, and how many seconds they had until impact.

But she was wrong.

It wasn't a comet. The mass burst into a thousand little pieces, and each of those slivers increased speed, heading directly toward them.

Nothing in nature acted like that.

Her heart sank as she understood what was about to happen. They were under attack.

In a daze, Nue didn't hear Rannn yelling orders. Her heart sank as she watched more and more comet-like masses headed in their direction before they burst all over the screen. The ship rocked, and red lights started to flash as alarms blared.

5

ATTACK

Rannn could feel Chollar in his head as he protected the ship by pushing away everything they could see on the scanners. There were thousands upon thousands of little hull drills. Small and compact with one purpose: to destroy.

Not something a pirate would use.

Whoever was doing this wanted them dead. The intricate way the drills worked said that they were probably of Fynbar's making. A defense maybe, against anyone trying to sneak to the planet via this large asteroid field.

He read the ship's distress log and knew it was only a matter of time before the pirate ship was no longer viable. They had already taken a hit from Fynbar's drones. Most spots had been fixed, but those temporary fixes would be destroyed.

Rannn needed to think of an escape plan, but he didn't have control over his mind or body at the moment. Chollar had taken over.

Rannn heard the bridge door slide open, but he couldn't look away from the screen. A body in an evo-suit crossed his periphery, holding something long and dark. Ansel's voice sounded modified through the speaker when he shouted, "Everyone's putting on an evo-suit. Lita and Sands say the drills have bioweapons. One of Fynbar's traps. Those drills breached the engine room and set off an alarm."

Bioweapons?

Did Fynbar even make bioweapons?

Rannn wanted everyone on the bridge so if there were a breach in the forward section of the ship, they could stay together. He hoped that Chollar heard his thoughts and would carry out his order.

Minutes later, the bridge was full of people.

Minutes after that, they were all dressed in evo-suits.

Chollar released Rannn's body as he stood over the visual and infrared screen, their only defense against the drills. Sci was by his side, both of them unspeaking, each moving his hands as if pushing the drills away.

The ship's emergency lights went on, and the alarm blared louder. The vessel's hull had been breached in three seconds. The ecosystem was winking out. The attacks kept coming, and Rannn stood unable to do anything but wait and hope that his Cerebrals kept them all alive.

THE ATTACK LASTED THREE HOURS.

The bridge was battered but whole, but the rest of the ship had been ruined. Chollar had used his telekinesis to remove the bridge from the rest of the spacecraft, making Rannn a witness to power unimaginable—even in Rannn's wildest dreams.

Currently, the Master Elder flew the ship via his power, using nothing mechanical.

Rannn had tied himself down next to the captain's chair to keep from floating into the walls. Yon tied himself next to

Chollar and made hand motions, probably giving piloting directions mentally rather than verbally.

The only electronic item working was the visual screen. And that only worked because Lita had brought her tool bag, which included a mini arc-reactor.

From the corner of his eye, Rannn saw Nue headed his way, grabbing on to everything she could to keep from floating. When she finally made it, she said, "The closest planet to where we were attacked is Angny. Are we going there?"

"Seth of Stars could walk onto this bridge and tell me to go there, and I'd spit in his face."

Nue paused for a moment, probably not used to any Yunkins slandering their god.

"You could have just said no."

They were past being polite to each other. She'd made it clear that she hated him. He wasn't going to play the fool and act like someone he wasn't. "It wouldn't express how much I hate that planet."

She was silent for a minute before she asked, "Why?"

Rannn watched Yon turn his head, probably waiting to see what he would say. It wasn't something any of them talked about. The summary was on the archives but, apparently, Nue was one of the very few who hadn't read his bio.

"Last time I was on that planet, I lost all my crew except Yon, Pax, and Ansel."

Yon turned around, and Rannn saw Yelena move closer but not touch her mate. Seconds later, Yon reached out and grabbed her hand. Rannn didn't know why it hit him so hard to see that, but he respected and envied it at the same time.

Yon had found a perfect mate. After everything his friend had been through, Yon had accomplished the one thing that every Yunkin male desired: a family and a *loving* partner.

"How did you lose them?" Nue asked.

Looking down so he could see her eyes, Rannn said, "The males were forced to fight in the pit. Each time was a fight to the death. The females...they were raped until they either died or killed themselves."

Rannn knew the moment Nue came to understand why he hated that planet. Her gaze darted down, and he saw her shrink a little.

Rannn figured he'd answered her question and was therefore done with the conversation. He had to think about the crew and what they were going to do now. Could the bridge last long enough to reach another planet, or would they get lucky and pass a ship?

When Nue looked back up, she wasn't looking at him anymore, she looked at the visual screen that Yon and Chollar were using to fly.

Chollar turned to look at Nue. "Jandy contacted Sasha to come and get us. Yon and I are not flying to anywhere in particular. We are trying to mimic flying space debris in case there are any other traps out there."

Nue moved closer to the console. "I remember seeing a moon just outside the asteroid belt. If we can land there, we could use its gravity to hold us until help arrives."

Yon and Yelena moved to give Nue more space.

Rannn watched as Nue spoke clearly and explained everything to Chollar as she went. This Nue was a professional and one who had a mind for navigation. It was a shame she didn't want to stay with the Federation.

He would have to look for someone with her skills to replace her. He liked having a brilliant-minded navigator who thought outside the box.

"How does Sasha even know where we are?" Nue asked, taking Rannn out of his mind.

Chollar answered. "Jandy is part Silk Demon, and she had a connection to Sasha."

"When you say a connection, do you mean that Jandy thorned Sasha?"

"Yes."

Nue was silent for a minute before she said, "If Sasha left Port Nicca right now, it would take about seven days for her to reach us from the spot we were attacked. From the moon, another few hours."

Chollar didn't look at her when he said, "You're worried we will die without food and water. But Ansel put medscopes in these evo-suits, and he says we are good for about ten days."

Rannn could hear her prolonged intake of breath. "He said that?"

"I heard his thoughts," Chollar said with a smirk.

Nue nodded and continued giving directions. With her back to him, Rannn could take her in and commit to memory the image of her at her best. She could have just let them all continue to sway in space, but she didn't. She acted with honor.

He hoped he never forgot this moment, even when she was long gone from his life. It was unfortunate that he would never get to know her better. He was genuinely attracted to her, had been from the start though he'd tried to ignore it, and he respected her abilities. While a relationship was impossible, he wondered if it could have been something special.

Too bad dreams were just that, dreams. And, sadly, he lived in reality.

6

ADVICE

It had been three days.

Nue sat strapped to the wall in a nearly constant state of mind-numbing boredom. Yon and Yelena slept in one corner, tied to each other and anchored to an outlet. Lita and Sands worked on something together.

They had arrived on the moon and were now awaiting their rescue. But the monotony was slowly draining away her sanity.

Not that she was the only one. Ansel was floating aimlessly through the bridge. She didn't know if he was sleeping or not. The only reason she knew he wasn't dead was because he apologized each time he bounced off someone.

Sci and Pax were playing a game they'd come up with where Sci tried to hit the Demon with a series of small metal objects, and Pax attempted to block them with a long, broken piece of chair.

Chollar stayed near the screen, keeping the ship anchored. His mate, Jandy, either stood next to him or tied herself to his side to sleep near him.

Every thirty-six hours, Lita's homemade alarm went off, letting everyone know when another day had passed.

Rannn only talked when someone asked him a question. From what Nue could tell, he hadn't moved or slept. She hated how much it bothered her that he wasn't sleeping. It wasn't good to stay up for so long.

She wasn't his mother or wife, and it wasn't her place. But, damn it, someone should say something.

Just then, Rannn started to tap the back of the chair. He looked around the bridge, stopping when he met Nue's eyes. "You doing okay?"

"Are you?" she asked back, floating a little bit.

Rannn watched her come closer before he clipped out, "I'm fine."

Sure, he was. "Is it weird that I'm thirsty but I don't *feel* thirsty. Like I miss drinking water."

Rannn faced forward as if he weren't going to answer. But then he said, "Me, too." She smiled to herself. This was probably Rannn being a captain. Stoic, silent, and grouchy.

THE RESCUE SHIP WAS SMALL. There were no extra rooms. It was a one-person vessel with one cleaner, a smaller galley, and a two-chair bridge. Nue and the rest of the crew were forced to squeeze into the cargo bay that was half the size of the bridge she'd spent the past five days in.

She tried desperately to be thankful for the food and water, but it felt like an extension of the hell she'd already experienced.

Mentally, she felt fatigued, even though she hadn't done anything.

She was pressed up between Yelena on her left and Jandy on her right. Rannn was on the other side of the cargo room. He talked to someone on his Minky screen that Sasha had brought him.

Absently, Nue mumbled to herself. "I don't think he's slept this whole time."

Yon, who was sitting next to Yelena, said, "He won't sleep until we're back on Garna. And even then, he will only sleep a few hours before dealing with the Sennites."

Sennites?

"What's *his* problem with the Sennites?" she asked.

"Have you not been listening to his conversations?"

"No, I can barely hear him," she said honestly.

Yon snorted. "The Sennites are dealing with a planet-wide disease, and they aren't allowing the Federation to help. Rannn is trying to make them see reason. But they aren't returning his messages. He's contacted Vivira to keep trying, hoping that a female might get them to see reason."

Nue felt a surge in her blood. A disease? Was it killing everyone? What was it doing?

As if coming out of a fog, she said, "The Sennites will not be interested in anything Vivra has to say."

"Why not?" Yon asked.

"Because she's acting under the direction of her captain. She can't enforce anything without Rannn's or the Federation's approval. Having her reach out would be a waste of time."

"Vivra is trying to help."

"How? Does she know how to cure the disease? The Sennites will only listen if you have something to give them."

"Well, that's why they're all going to die. Because they're too stupid to ask for assistance."

Yon was a foul-mouthed jerk. Everyone knew that. Even Nue. So, she tried not to get upset. She reminded herself that cursing at him would do nothing. She also recalled that voicing her opinion was pointless. Yon wasn't the captain, and even if he was, he wouldn't consider her opinions worth noting.

Nue tried to keep her mouth closed.

Tried and failed. "Says the Yunkin who practically died in a Numan lab because he refused to call down for help."

She felt the silence in the cargo room grow. For some reason, her eyes found the captain to see how pissed off he was by her comment. Nue rarely spoke to any of the crewmembers. Mostly because she had been trying to hide her arrest record.

There was no reason for her to be so outspoken now, but she couldn't help it. She was stressed.

Oddly enough, when she looked, the side of Rannn's mouth was curled.

Wait, what did that mean?

"She's got you there, Yon," Pax said. She hadn't even known he was listening in on their conversation.

"Shut up, Pax," Yon said and then leveled his gaze on her. "All right, *navigator,* do you have anything helpful to add?"

It felt like a trap. Like he was willing to tell Rannn what she said and ask him to do it, just so he could throw it back in her face later. Despite her internal reasoning, she told him, "Yeah, I do. Firstly, if Vivra contacts the Sennite admiral to instruct her on what she *was commanded* to do, she'll likely remove her from communications immediately."

"Why?" Yon asked, moving his mate from his lap to his side so he could look at Nue.

"Think of it like this...if another female comes into your house telling you how to take care of your kids, you instantly hate her. And there is no forgiveness for that kind of rudeness."

Rannn spoke up. "I had Clalls send that message."

"Oh." Nue chuckled. "That's different. All he has to do is apologize, and she will promptly forgive him."

She saw both Yon's and Rannn's confusion, so she elaborated. "Ugly males are easy to forgive. The uglier they are, the cuter they come off....at least, to Sennites."

That didn't seem to help.

"That makes no sense," Yon said, disgusted.

"Sennites think all males are stupid. It makes sense," Rannn said in a tone that Nue didn't like.

"No," Nue said firmly. "Not all males are forgiven so easily. It's specifically the ugly ones. Night Demons are so ugly, Sennites think they're cute. Before the Federation, Night Demons were known to be pets and companions to high-ranking Sennite rulers."

"Are you serious?" Pax asked, drawing her attention from the two Yunkins, who seemed to be having a difficult time digesting what she said.

Pax looked amused.

"Yes. Clalls would be highly favored because of his deformity. Add in that he's clever, and he would be worth a lot of money back in the day. In fact, if Clalls is there during the negotiations, Vivra will likely get better Sennite cooperation."

For whatever reason, Nue looked at Chollar, wondering why he hadn't told them all the truth. The Cerebral snorted. "Despite your accusations, I do have manners."

Did he?

"You're a Sennite," Rannn said as if he just figured it out.

"She doesn't look like a Sennite. No purple hair or eyes," Yon countered.

Holding up a piece of her midnight-black hair, she said, "Nara's polymer hair color. It will stay this shade until I pay an inordinate amount of money to get the polymer out." Then she pointed at her eyes, which were a silvery grey-blue hue. "Oriso contacts. They last five years."

Why was she telling everyone this?

"Would negotiations go better if *you* were the negotiator?" Rannn asked.

"No. Not with my background."

Rannn frowned. "I will have your charges expunged before long."

Nue bit her lip for a moment, not wanting to confess too much. "It has nothing to do with that," she said, hoping that would be enough.

Rannn kept his eyes on her, but he didn't pry.

Interesting.

"What does that mean?" Yon asked.

Rannn spoke up instead. "Means you can all shut up so I can tell Vivra and Clalls the new plan."

Yon kept his eyes on her expectantly. She didn't answer him because she didn't have to. Rannn had made it pretty damn clear he was taking her side.

And that...roused a feeling of victory within her. Damn if she understood why, especially considering that she was supposed to still hate him.

7

AT LAST

Garna. Finally.

Rannn walked out of the shower when he heard a double knock at the door. Assuming it was Yon or Pax, he called, "Come in." He'd hoped to catch up on some messages and then rest, but he would see what they had to say first.

The door from his office to his captain's cabin opened, and in walked Nue. Her eyes widened at the sight of his naked chest for a moment before she schooled her expression. Rannn had assumed that she might turn around or offer to come back when he was dressed, but instead, she said, "You said to come in."

That he had. Considering that they had shared a cabin for weeks in the Outworlds, he didn't care that she saw his scars. She had seen them before. "What do you want?"

"I wanted to let you know I am not going to leave the Garna. Just in case you already talked with someone about shipping me somewhere."

He nodded to let her know that he heard, but he wondered why she hadn't just sent him the message. Why had she come in person? Then, he remembered that he had terminated her

Federation ID, and there was no other way for her to communicate with him. Interestingly, he didn't think anybody outside of his small group of friends would just walk into his cabin.

Did that mean she was comfortable here?

Rannn wasn't sure if he liked the idea of that or not. It wasn't like anything could happen between them. Yes, she was beautiful—he'd thought so the first time he saw her—which was why he had struggled so much when he found out that she was a murderer. Or assumed to be. But she'd made it crystal clear that she didn't like him. And even if she did, he had been taught that it was the highest honor to only share physical intimacies with a wife.

Noticing Nue's expectant expression, he told her, "I haven't made arrangements. I'll hold off until you say otherwise."

"Thank you."

He nodded again, expecting her to leave. She did not.

Nue scanned the room, and he wondered if she wanted to say something else, or if she was inspecting the space in that way females did.

He grabbed a pair of underwear from his cabinet. He didn't bother to warn Nue that he was removing his towel. If she looked, that was on her. And it would let her know that he wasn't going to be delicate around her.

Dropping the terrycloth, he went about getting dressed. His shirt being the last thing he pulled on. When he finally turned, Nue was leaning against the table, smirking appreciatively.

He should have sent her out.

Why was he allowing this?

"What do you want, Nue?"

"I noticed that my profile has been updated on the ship, as well as my Federation disciplinary record."

Sitting on his bed, he pulled his boots from under the rack and shoved his right foot inside. "I told you I would get that cleared. As well as release you from duty." Rannn didn't like that she doubted him. But then again, she was a Sennite, and that race was matriarchal. It was possible she believed she was inherently smarter than him simply because he was male.

"So you did."

Rannn put on his other boot, wondering if she was trying to say thank you, or if she had come for something else. This was not a social visit by a friend or a personal visit by a crewmember. This was Nue...being odd.

Dressed and ready, he stood up, walked to the door, and pointed for her to exit first. She walked out, still not really saying what she had come for. He knew there was more than she'd said.

Considering that he had yet to sleep, he was too tired to pull it out of her. If she had something to say, she could say it. Otherwise, she could just...shadow him for all he cared.

He shut the door that connected his office and his cabin. Nue moved over to the wall side of the table, still not saying anything. He wondered belatedly if she knew about the meeting that was happening soon.

The door to his office opened, and Ansel walked in just as one of Rannn's Minky screens pinged on the wall. It was the meeting alert that he had set but then forgot about because he was just too tired.

"Just in time," he lied to the doctor. As he moved to the screen to answer the call, he told Nue, "If you're going to stay, take a seat on the other side." Having her here might be a good idea.

Ansel took his place near the Minky's camera. Rannn accepted the call and stood next to the doctor.

Vivra, Clalls, and a Sennite who Rannn assumed was the planet's admiral, Livanna, were on the other side of the screen.

Livanna was the first to speak. "Now that everyone is here, I think it's best to speak plainly. I am not pleased to be maneu-

vered into cooperation. This is my planet, and I will not,"—
Livanna glared at the camera—"be instructed in how to take
care of my people. Especially by a low-ranking captain."

Before Rannn could respond, Vivra said, "We are here to
help you. If you don't want my help, I have better things to do."

Rannn heard Nue exhale, and knew that Vivra was coming
on way too strong. But it wasn't an act, it was just the way
Vivra was.

Even Clalls cut his eyes at Vivra as if silently scolding her.

Rannn wondered if following Nue's advice was actually a
good idea. So far, not so good. Trying to respectfully smooth
things over, he said, "Whatever resources you need, I will make
sure you get them. My doctor, Ansel, is the best physician you'll
find in the Federation. He can help and will take direction from
you."

"We have our own doctors," Livanna said before addressing
Vivra. "And by all means, return to whatever is more important,
Bolark."

"Happily," Vivra said with her chin in the air. As she started
to walk away, Rannn noticed that Clalls had not moved.

Vivra noticed too, then stopped and glared at him.

This seemed to please Livanna. "Demon loyalties are cheap.
You should have known that, Bolark."

Clalls smiled. "Vivra's just upset that she had to leave Garna
to come here instead of meeting her mate, who just arrived on
the ship. So, when she said she had better things to do...she
meant it literally. Him. Get it?"

Vivra's scales darkened.

Livanna outright smiled. "Ah, how long has her mate been
away?"

"Months," Clalls said with exasperation.

Livanna chuckled and then waved a hand at Vivra. "Understandable, child. By all means, return to your mate."

"Clalls," Vivra hissed. "I'm going to kill you."

"I love you, too. Kisses and all that. And tell your Red Demon about that thing I did for you that one time."

Vivra was practically shaking, and Rannn honestly figured there was a fifty-fifty chance she would kill him right there on the spot. If he were Vivra, he would have at least shot a phaser at Clalls for discussing his personal life.

"She's mated to a Red Demon?" Livanna said with a healthy dose of scandalous interest.

Clalls' eyes rolled, and he whispered loudly, "I know. Disgusting, right? I have no idea what she sees in him. He's just one big ball of muscle. No brains."

That seemed to make Livanna smirk. "Well, we all have our weaknesses."

"Do we?" Clalls said, fully turning his attention on the admiral. "I'll tell you mine, if you tell me yours."

Livanna chuckled. "Doubtful, Demon. You'd use it against me."

"Perhaps," he said in a silky way, and Rannn had no idea why that made the Sennite blush.

Rannn was about to bring the topic back around when Nue cleared her throat softly. He turned to see her shake her head.

Clalls continued. "Peaches, I'm going to make you a deal. If you give our doc a chance to fix your little baby-making problem, for let's say...a week, then I will personally take care of that problem you had last year."

Livanna's eyes widened.

Clalls mouthed a word Rannn didn't see.

"How do you know?"

"I have my ways. What do you say, Peaches?"

Silence. Then, "You have yourself a deal." Livanna looked at the screen. "I expect you down here with the doctor in an hour. I will have my medical staff debrief you."

"That won't be possible," Ansel began, but Clalls cut him off.

"He's got all his stuff in his lab. It's probably easier if he video chats with your team. Don't need to spread the virus or anything. Especially since it's airborne."

At that, Rannn looked over to Nue, worried that if it was a Sennite disease, it might affect her.

"How did you know?" Livanna said.

"Because it's planet-wide. How else would it be transmitted?" Clalls said incredulously.

"Very clever, Demon. And that would be perfectly fine."

The call ended after a quick goodbye. Rannn stopped Ansel with a hand. "If there's a disease on that planet, Clalls and Vivra could carry it back here and infect the crew."

"I know. Why do you think I sent them down there? I have the containment lab under the ship. Vivra will stay in there as I take samples and run tests. Pax is already waiting for her."

"And Clalls?" Rannn asked.

"He's staying on the planet to do what Demons do best," Nue said, rising from the chair. "Let me guess, he's going to get more dirt for you?"

Ansel barely gave her a glance. "If you mean data, then yes. I need to know everything so I can come up with a cure. If you think I care about their political aspirations, then you're wrong."

Ansel gave him a look as if to say, *Why is she even here?*

Rannn didn't answer, and Ansel likely knew he wouldn't. Because Rannn rarely explained himself.

When the doctor left, he debated asking Nue to leave, as well.

Instead, she broke the silence with, "Because I have been removed from Federation duty, I don't have a job."

"You haven't taken any tests. Legally, I can't just award you a position."

"You could have said I was a FAVVI."

"You still would have to take the tests. Is that what you want? To be a part of the crew?"

She pursed her lips. "No, not really."

Rannn set his arm on top of his chair. "Didn't think so."

"I could be a consultant. Federation people consult from time to time."

Hmm. "Yon is my XO. I would go to him if I wanted to discuss options."

"Non-Yunkin," she said as she leaned back in her seat.

"Then I would talk to Pax, Ansel, or Sci."

"Those are all men," she countered as if she were upset with him. He understood what she was trying to do, so he deliberately added, "Vivra makes some good points. She's a great commander."

"Is she? Because from what I just saw, Clalls closed that negotiation. One that I suggested."

Was she looking for a thank you? "You're a guest on the Garna. Not a liaison, or counsel, or anything else. You want to be a part of the team, you apply to the Federation. You don't, that's fine. If you're here looking for an extension to my apology by way of a favor, that's not happening."

"Trust me, I wasn't here to beg for a favor."

Finally. "Then what did you want?"

"To ask if you planned to investigate my old case."

Ah.

"Nue," he started, but she held up her hand to stop him.

She didn't get to say a word because his Minky screen pinged with an incoming call. It was a voice call from his cousin.

He held up his finger, asking for her to wait. Answering the call from his Minky desk, he said, "Orin, what is it?"

"I'm letting you know I'm taking leave."

"What?"

"Yeah. I know you don't take leave, but I need one. My wife and I need a break."

Rannn paused for a moment. "Is everything okay?"

"No. It's not. But it's my marriage, and I will deal with it."

At that, Rannn folded his arms with disappointment. "Are you taking off because you want to? Or does she want you to?"

"I'm not discussing my personal life with you."

"Okay," Rannn said, wondering who had been caught cheating. It wasn't something any Yunkin talked about because they were all supposed to be honorable, but things happened. Rannn just hoped it wasn't Orin, or he'd kick his cousin's ass.

While Rannn was quiet, Orin added, "By the way, a Commander Ettom challenged your pardon for your crewmember. He brought his concerns to the admiral council and is demanding that you prove, with evidence, that she didn't do it."

Out of the corner of his eye, Rannn saw Nue drop her head forward.

"I'm in the middle of a planet-wide epidemic with the Sennites. I'll have Ansel take her samples and have them escorted by a guard to the Yunkin labs to verify."

"What? The Sennites have a planet-wide epidemic? When did this happen?"

"Supposedly, it's been happening for over a year. I have Ansel working on it now, getting the specifics. I'll send an update in a few hours."

Orin cursed. "You know what? Just take care of this and send me a report when it's all done. I can't talk anymore. I have to go."

Rannn felt a smidge sympathetic for his cousin. "I always take care of it."

"Bye," Orin said as he terminated the call. Silence consumed the room. Ignoring the awkwardness, Rannn sent a message to Pax.

Get your best security officer to take some samples to Yunkin.

Then he closed that message and ignored the long list of messages with the subject: *marriage proposals*.

Dialing Ansel's number, he let it go to one ring before he decided to walk Nue to medical himself.

"Come on, we need to get your samples."

As soon as they were in the hall, Nue said, "You have a lot of marriage proposals."

Inhaling, he ignored her statement. He needed to sleep. He could feel the strain on his body and eyes. And the last thing he wanted to do was discuss *that*.

Nue stayed quiet and followed his lead.

Thank, Seth.

AN HOUR LATER, Officer Shady was flying an automated transport to Yunkin with the samples. As soon as they made the comparison, they would know that it wasn't Nue, and Rannn's promise would be kept.

Rannn and Nue walked into Shady's office. Nue didn't need to follow him anymore, but Rannn was too tired to tell her to go back to her room.

Eventually, she'd figure it out.

When the office door opened, Rannn sluggishly turned around to see who it was, but no one was there. His reflexes were slow, and he'd assumed the door slider malfunctioned. Then a delivery pod floated in. A small hole opened up, followed by a soft *pfft,* and he knew it was too late.

He looked down to see the end of the dart. The butt end had a small silver tube the size of a thumbnail.

It happened so fast, he didn't have time to react.

Beside him, he heard Nue yelp. She had an identical dart in her chest. His body felt sluggish, but he used the last of his energy to grab Nue, remove the dart, and push her into his cabin to stop whoever was trying to kidnap them.

He didn't black out like he expected, though.

Instead, his stomach burned and bubbled. His knees hit the floor with a loud thunk. His insides roiled, and before he knew it, blood flew from his mouth.

8

ILLNESS

Nue fell on her hands and knees after being pushed inside Rannn's cabin. Behind her, she turned to see the captain holding one palm to the door, and the other on the floor as he vomited copious amounts of grey blood.

What the hell was happening?

"Rannn," she said, reaching for him. Her stomach gave a quick squeeze, and then it lurched as if she'd drunk a gallon of acid.

"Ra—" Nue tried again, but as she opened her lips, she watched yellow blood eject from her mouth. It went on and on without stopping.

Her eyes teared up, and she was sure she would suffocate if she didn't stop.

She was on her third or fourth session, her arms buckling, and was starting to get lightheaded when a blur of white moved around her. She felt pressure at her waist, then something slipped up her shirt, and a wet hand pressed a hard thing to her chest right under her boob.

She shook as another wave took her, but she couldn't feel anymore. Her stomach squeezed and burned, but nothing came up, and she was able to suck in blood-tinged air for the first time in many seconds—or minutes.

Time moved strangely.

Sucking in another harsh breath, she noticed that Rannn was no longer by the door. A streak of grey blood moved from that spot to her, and she didn't care to ask how. She was just thankful that she wasn't vomiting anymore.

"Just keep breathing. The medscope should take care of it."

Medscope?

"You just...had one...lying around?"

"In...my chest," he said between breaths.

At that, she sat up and turned around to see Rannn's ghastly-looking face, and below that, a huge, bleeding chest wound. Rannn grabbed her arm, pulled her back into his legs, and then pressed the medscope to her stomach. "You need to heal, Nue. Stop moving...around."

"You're bleeding out," she said, feeling nauseous, but not as severely as before.

"I'll be fine," he said as he slowly blinked. And then his eyes rolled back in his head, and he slumped over, vomiting again.

Nue took the medscope that dropped to the floor and placed it on his midsection. As she held it there, she could feel her stomach begin to gurgle, and not in a good way. Breathing out of her mouth, she prayed to Seth of Stars that it would heal Rannn before she had to use it on herself again.

Six hours.

That's how long it took. By the time things quieted, Nue was exhausted and surrounded by filth that she refused to think about. She lay on her side, feeling like she was in a nightmare and unable to wake up.

Rannn was on the floor next to her with a hand on her hip.

His wound had healed last. She was amazed that he was still alive with all of the blood he'd lost.

Numbly, she asked, "Why was it in your chest?"

"Huh?"

"Why did you have a medscope in your chest?"

"Ansel put it in before we reached Keagan. Wanted the extra backup in case I needed it but couldn't use my hands to get it. Like being tied up or something."

Ah. That made sense.

"We need to get off this floor and shower," Rannn said without moving.

She agreed, but she didn't move either. Her body felt nearly drained of life. "Okay."

"You can go first."

"No, thanks. I doubt I can stand up."

Rannn didn't say anything for several moments. "I can hold you up if you need help."

She almost smiled but couldn't muster the energy. "Are you offering to shower with me?"

"I guess I am."

Nue didn't have a chance to respond. Rannn grabbed her waist and lifted her up, then very slowly moved her across the bed. He used the mattress for support when they moved too fast.

Inside the cleaner, Nue tried to take off her own clothes, but she could barely lift her arms. So, Rannn did that for her, too.

"You should be weaker than I am. You lost a lot of blood," she said with self-loathing that she didn't have the strength to examine.

"Don't pout," he said, unfastening her pants and pulling them down. "Step out."

She did. Then he ushered her into the cleaner, sat her down, and undressed himself. If she weren't so exhausted, she might have felt uncomfortable being naked in a shower with him. But he wasn't showing any signs of excitement.

The water was cold when he started it, and she hissed. Rannn held an arm around her waist, keeping her steady, and used his other hand to begin rinsing her hair.

By the end of her shower, she was on her knees, bent over with Rannn washing and rinsing her hair because it really did take two hands. Then he moved her around like a rag doll as he washed her body.

When he finished, he let her sit as he quickly cleaned himself.

Again, she was too weak to feel anything, but that didn't stop her from watching his manhood for any sign of interest.

"Nue," Rannn said, gaining her eyes. "Stop."

For a few seconds she did, then she found herself looking again. "Why is it so dark?"

Rannn groaned. "Because Yunkin blood is grey, and our skin is pale. It's nothing but muscle and blood. That's what it looks like."

That made sense, but seriously... "It looks so out of place."

"Since we're not sex partners, it really doesn't matter if you're put off by it."

She wasn't put off at all. But she didn't tell him that.

"Abstaining until you're married? Are you having a hard time picking a partner? Is that why there are so many unanswered offers?" She had been dying to know more about this, but she figured there was no way in hell he would answer. Especially after he'd shut it down hours ago.

But on the floor, naked, looking disheveled as hell, she found that she didn't care about politeness. She wanted to know.

"I'm a widower. Those offers are from people looking to use my status to add to theirs. *That's* why I don't answer them." His voice was hard.

Possibly a warning.

Looking at his manhood again, Nue thought that it would be an awful waste if he didn't have sex again. He probably knew how to please someone well.

She wanted to find out.

"Staring at it won't change its color," Rannn said as he turned off the water.

She wanted to tell him that it was okay and that it didn't make him look unappealing, but she didn't get a chance.

Rannn grabbed a towel and dried her off, a little too roughly. The cabin didn't smell as bad as she remembered. Until she saw a little black metal ball rolling across the floor and understood why. "Mini duro cleaners," she said, recognizing the icon.

"Worth every kelep."

Rannn sat her on his bed. "You're to stay here while the crew finds the shooter."

She nodded and tried to fall back onto the bed. She didn't care about anything but getting under the covers. It took Rannn pulling the blankets from under her first before she was able to get in.

"Do you want me to get you some clothes?"

"Shhhhhh. Mommy's sleeping." She had no idea why she'd called herself Mommy, but at this point, she didn't care.

The bed dipped behind her, and she knew who it was. She waited until he was next to her to say the last thought she could muster. "Thank you for saving me."

He grunted.

Closing her eyes, Nue felt safe. It was the craziest thing because, just a week ago, she wouldn't have believed that she could say that about Rannn. But everything had changed. All those times he'd made her want to scream and kill him were gone.

Rannn was the same male, yet not. She didn't have the

mental capacity to explain it to herself, but she knew that in those hours of sickness and fear, she'd found respect *and* safety with him.

Before dropping off to sleep, she felt the light pressure of lips against her head.

He was *kissing* her.

Her heart warmed with the thought of being on the right side of a male like Rannn.

9

EMERGENCY

Rannn woke up with warmth against his side. He stretched and rolled away from it, seeking the cool side of the bed. He settled in for a few seconds before the warmth followed and snaked around his torso and leg.

More awake now, he lifted the blue blanket and saw a thin, light brown arm. Turning around, he saw a sea of black hair and Nue's pouty face. "Stop moving," she muttered.

Something fluttered in his blood. A lightness that he didn't understand. He could feel the sides of his mouth attempting to pull up into a smile.

Why hadn't he known she was so cute when she slept?

He rested his head back on the pillow, letting the last remaining claws of deep sleep unhook themselves. Once he was fully awake, he remembered why she was in his bed. He also remembered that they were both naked.

He needed to get up, check the time and see if his crew had found the shooter. But he hesitated because...he just did.

He wanted this memory because he doubted he would ever have the chance to be here again—next to her, feeling her warmth and witnessing how she clung to him like she was desperate to be close.

He wished against logic that he could have this for the rest of his life, but he knew he couldn't. He had a duty to his race. To marry and breed with a Yunkin female. To carry on his bloodline.

But he wished against logic that Seth of Stars could make it happen. Because he had never woken up feeling like this. Feeling *right* with someone.

Nue stirred, pushing him to his back and snuggling closer. She lifted a knee over his legs and stretched her hand over his chest. But then she moved it too far down and skimmed his morning stiffness. Until she moved back up and grabbed it fully.

Rannn felt the air leave his lungs.

Nue stilled, and he knew she was awake.

Her beautiful, metallic greyish-blue eyes opened. Even though they were contacts, they were still beautiful. She immediately looked down to where her hand was under the blanket. She dropped her hold and scrambled back.

He expected her to freak out that she was naked, but her mouth opened with an apology instead. "I am so sorry. I didn't mean to touch you inappropriately."

Was he a skem for liking it?

He flashed her a look of *too late now* and moved off the bed. Walking to the clothes cabinet, he heard, "Wait, Rannn?"

He turned, and her eyes darted to his manhood. She smiled. "I just wanted to see how big it got."

For the love of Seth, did she want to bed him? Because if she kept talking like that, he was going to do it—regardless of the consequences.

"Wrong color, but big enough?" he heard himself ask.

Nue crawled out of bed, taking the blanket with her and

wrapping it around her breasts. "The color's fine, big guy. But it's how you use it that determines if you're the right fit."

"Shut up, Nue." Wiping his face, he tried to control the rush of desire that rocketed through him. Still, he could do nothing except wholly accept that he was full and ready to lay her back on the bed—and take her violently. But he was a Yunkin, damn it. He could control those urges.

Mercifully, she moved away from him and into the kitchenette, rummaging through his packs of food.

Pulling out his clothes, he dressed and used the cleaner. On his way to his office, he saw her nibbling on a nutrient bar while sitting on the counter. "Have fun at work."

In his office, he waited until the door had shut before he closed his eyes and tried to clear his thoughts and relieve the pressure of his need.

Blitzing would backfire. She was a Sennite. They didn't marry or mate. They had bed partners, but that was it. And he'd be damned if he allowed himself to know her body just to have it taken away whenever she was done with him.

Feeling the pressure ebb, he adjusted his pants and moved to the Minky table to check how late it was.

At first, he didn't understand what the calendar read. But when he checked his Minky screen, it mirrored the same numbers.

"Holy, Seth," he whispered. It had been two days.

He initiated a video call to Yon.

Yon answered on the first ring. "You're finally awake. Hold on, let me put you on the Minky screen."

Rannn waited. When the video reconnected, he saw that Yon was in medical, standing next to Ansel.

"Everything's gone to hell, so prepare," Yon warned gravely.

Rannn raised his brows, not worried that he wouldn't be able to take the debrief. "Can't be worse than Angny. And I contacted

Sci and Chollar the second I was shot, so I doubt it's as bad as you're making it out to be."

Yon had an odd look on his face. "I don't use Angny as a baseline. But to each their own." It was a cut and a chastisement, and Rannn could respect it. But Angny was the worst that he had ever experienced, so it *was* the baseline for him.

"Did you catch the shooter?"

"Of course, we did," Yon answered. "It was a delivery pod, not hard to catch. Sands and Lita are trying to find out who sent it. And who manufactured it."

"Whoever sent it must have known I just got back. But that information is Federation-sealed." Meaning, the culprit was Federation.

"Whoever sent it didn't just shoot you. It also dispersed something else. The biohazard alarm went off on your level. Minutes later, it went off on the lower levels, too."

What?

"Per protocol, I evacuated the crew in sections to try and keep the spread of the disease to a minimum."

"What disease?" Rannn asked, feeling an odd sensation cramping his forearms.

It was probably just nerves.

"Ansel is taking samples and analyzing the vents now. He isolated a virus, but he doesn't know what it is."

Rannn rubbed his mouth at that. What if this was another Eldon disease, and his entire crew was infected? He shuddered at the thought. "Are you and Ansel the only ones on Garna?"

"No. Yelena and I are here with Ansel, Sci, Sasha, and their daughter, Amaree. We're in medical."

Rannn could see Yon's stress in his neck as he talked. The male must have been thinking the same thing. They were all infected.

Yon continued. "Pax and Vivra are still in the lab under the ship. Their tests came back clean, but I think they are safer there than being back on board."

"Sands is on the other ship?"

"Sands and Lita are walking around in evo-suits, working on the delivery pod. They were able to suit up before the alarm went off on their level. Most of those who might be infected are the officers, and they are on a single ship piloted by Sol."

With honest fervor, Rannn hoped that his officers weren't all infected. He did not want them all to die a gruesome death.

"Very good, Yon." And it was. Yon was a very capable male. Rannn was pissed that his first mate would never get the chance to run his own ship or show the admirals just how reliable and honorable he was.

The male had done the unpardonable. He'd demanded a divorce from a wife who'd left the marriage bed to beg her father to let her come back and live with him because she felt disgusted being married to a Yunkin-Demon hybrid.

In Rannn's mind, Yon had been honorable to release her. But, Yon being Yon, he didn't sugarcoat the situation and thus offended her family, thereby causing him to be exiled from the planet from that moment on.

His excellent Federation career saved him from being discharged. Rannn, of course, respected the hell out of the male.

"Also, I tried to update Orin about what was going on, but he didn't answer," Yon said.

Remembering the last conversation he'd had with his cousin, Rannn said, "Orin's on personal leave."

Ansel stepped into the video camera. "For what?"

"Personal things," Rannn said dryly, keeping his cousin's confidence regarding his marital life. "By the way, are you going to come and get samples to find out what Nue and I were shot with? I had assumed we would have been moved into a medbed or something."

"You were shot with arsenice," Ansel said quickly. "While you were sleeping, I went in and got samples from both you and Nue. I was in an evo-suit, and we have quarantined all levels so I think you should stay there until I can figure this out."

Rannn forced himself to stay still. "When will you know what the disease is?" Because he didn't like the idea of anyone dying suddenly from an unknown virus.

"Soon," the doctor said with sincerity.

"Do you think it was Calum?"

Ansel shrugged. "I'm not ruling it out."

Rannn thought about that for a moment and hated the idea that he was living the last few days of his life. Peering at the door between his office and his cabin, he dreaded what they would suffer if this *was* something from Calum.

The only thing he was pleased about was that he would be with Nue until the end.

Seth of Stars...was it really the end for him?

And was he really thinking about a female in his possible last moments? An infuriating one, at that—albeit beautiful.

10

MISSED OPPORTUNITY

Nue watched the door, expecting Rannn to come back in. The way he had been hard for her made her certain he would.

But it had been over forty minutes, and still, the Yunkin didn't walk back in to take her on the counter. She had felt her wetness as she sat thinking about Rannn's body against hers.

Huffing, she shoved off the counter, unraveled her blanket, and threw it on the bed. If Rannn wasn't going to take care of her, she would take matters into her own hands. And then, she'd make sure he regretted not coming back.

Because she couldn't have been clearer that she was interested in a blitz. Hell, at this point, she was ready for a hundred of them.

Rannn returned to his cabin to see the blanket on the bed and to hear the shower running. So, he grabbed a package of food and ripped it open, unsure what to do about the possible gruesome future. He needed to tell Nue. She deserved to know what was going on and settle her affairs in case this *was* the end.

Just as he brought the open end of the pouch to his mouth, he heard a moan coming from the cleaner.

He set the food down, ignoring that it'd tipped over, and walked purposely towards the source of the noise.

There it was again. Low, lusty, and feminine.

That couldn't be because she was enjoying the warmth of the water. She had to be...

Stepping back, his stomach clenched at the thought of her taking care of herself. Good Seth, he was stunned. Why would she...?

Rannn stood still, not feeling so much dread as more of an uncharacteristic desire to join her. To be the one to take care of her.

"Yessss," she said huskily. His sex woke up again.

He lifted his hand to open the door and walk in, but then he sobered. If he joined her now, she might be too embarrassed to finish, and there was no point in cutting her short. The least he could do was let her finish.

The water stopped abruptly, and he was finally able to breathe deeply. Holy hell, had he been holding his breath the entire time?

He needed to leave. There was no reason for her to know that he'd heard. There was no honor in embarrassing her.

But as he exited the cabin, his mind replayed her soft mewling and imagined what it would be like to have her. He didn't stop when he entered the office.

He strode right into the long, empty hall. In one fluid motion, he reached back and struck the wall. The bang echoed in his ears and reverberated down his arm. The instant flash of pain didn't calm his growing frustrations.

Rannn leaned his head against the cool grey walls. He needed to control himself. He needed to get a handle on his need.

The images in his mind didn't stop. His need continued growing until his shaft rose, heavy and full.

What he wouldn't do to walk back into his cabin and blitz Nue until neither of them could stand up. What would it be like to empty his seed inside her, fulfilling his most secret fantasy?

He was stronger than his lust. He was a captain, and his crew needed him. He had to remember that.

Pushing away from the wall, he spoke to himself. "Honor above all else."

And blitzing Nue wouldn't bring honor to him or to her.

Rannn waited until he had sufficiently calmed down before he returned to the office, his knuckles throbbing slightly.

Inside the office, the Minky table pinged with a voice call from Ansel.

"Ansel," he greeted as he accepted the call.

"I wanted to give you a quick update."

"On the Sennite problem?"

"No. I have not been able to get ahold of the Federation's head doctor. I wanted to update him on the potential bio threat. When I couldn't get him on a call, I tried calling your mother, and she didn't answer any of her work or home IDs."

Rannn stood up, but barely. His mother *always* answered. "How long ago did you try?"

"Minutes."

Holding up a finger, Rannn said, "I'm going to call her at home." He moved to the second Minky screen and punched in an ID number that he knew by heart. It didn't make a single ring. An error popped up on his screen that said the network was down.

"Says the quantum network is offline." It shouldn't be. Yunkin was the hub for all ship-wide quantum communications.

Rannn tried again.

Same error.

Again.

Same error.

He scrolled his contacts and found Clalls' ID. Hitting the call button, he waited. On the second ring, the Demon answered.

"In the middle of something, Cap."

"I don't care what you're doing. Your new priority is to get ahold of my mother."

There was a pause. A second later, the voice call turned into a video one. Clalls' expression was schooled. "You want me to call your mother? And this is important...why?"

"No calls are going through. It says the quantum network is down. There's a potential virus on the ship. The Federation's head doctor needs to know. My mother needs to know. Something happened, and you have the skills to find out what."

Clalls huffed. "Flattery will get you everywhere. Fine. I'll do it. But in return..."

Rannn could feel his muscles flex in his arm as he pointed at the screen. "I'm your captain, this is an order. There is no deal to settle on."

Clalls rolled his eyes. "No, Captain, I was thinking that you would instead promote me to commander. I feel confident that I deserve it after this particular mission."

That, he could do. "When this mission is over, I'll think about it."

Clalls smiled. "Perfect. I'll let you know what I find out in the next thirty-six hours."

Rannn didn't want to wait a whole day. "Try to make it sooner."

"No promises," Clalls said before terminating the call.

Rannn stood tall and firm, desperately trying to calm his anxiety. His mom was fine. The only reason she wasn't answering was because she couldn't.

On the other screen, Ansel gave him five seconds of silence. "You know, I didn't think Clalls was going to be such a valuable officer. And yet...he has a particular skill set worth admiring."

"I recognized it from back when we dealt with Eldon," Rannn said, feeling the small throb in his knuckles extend up to his forearm. Oddly, the other arm was cramping again, too.

Nue exited the shower feeling good and a little drained. Maybe a bit swollen with how hard she'd taken care of herself. But the end results were worth it.

Using the towel on her hair, she caught a red goo dripping off the counter. Changing direction from the bed to the kitchenette, she saw the package of food slumped over, the contents dribbling out.

She hadn't left that there.

Her stomach dropped as she looked at the cabin door. Covering her mouth, she cursed. "He heard me." There was no other reason for Rannn to leave food on the counter. She had been his cabin mate for weeks, and he was very clean.

Nue cursed again. How would she ever face him?

Wait.

Why was she fretting? She wanted this. She *wanted* him to know what he did to her. Smiling, she left the food package and headed to the office door, wearing only her towel. Letting it slip close to the edge of her breast, she waited for the door to open.

Rannn's head tilted, but he didn't look her in the eyes. "Yes?"

Yes? That was how he was going to address what'd

happened? He was just going to pretend it *didn't* happen? Oh no, he wasn't.

"I don't have anything to wear."

"You can borrow my clothes."

"Or I can go to my room and get my own."

Rannn looked at his Minky table again, skimming a message, ignoring her near-complete nakedness. "Not in my towel, you're not."

Oh. Was that how it was? Snidely, she said, "Afraid someone will think something of it if I walk around in *your* towels? Heaven forbid anyone thinks you sank so low."

She watched him flex his hand and then turn his wrist as if he wanted to punch something. Good, she was glad he was mad. Because she was, too. How dare he save her life then act like she was unworthy of his affections.

Jerk.

Rannn sat back as if exasperated. Using his legs, he turned the chair to face her, legs out, looking all sorts of yummy. She totally resented it.

"I meant, you're not walking the halls in a towel because there is a possible biohazard on the ship, and we are quarantined to my cabin. You may use my clothes in the meantime."

His tone was too controlled, and it reminded her how Yunkin he was and how much she didn't like overly controlled Yunkins.

Part of her wanted to drop the towel and walk away to make sure he got a good view. But she wasn't pathetic like that. She wasn't going to try and seduce him with a blatant look at her body.

She would seduce him into wanting her. All of her. And then he would beg her to stay with him.

Even though he was a Yunkin. Males were still...male.

With mocking sincerity, she said, "Thanks. I'll see if you have anything that fits."

Rannn didn't stop her or say anything when she turned around and walked back into the room. As soon as the door had shut, she ripped off the towel and threw it onto the floor. Stupid Yunkin had utterly ruined her good mood.

Ugh.

13

CHOLLAR DEBRIEF

Rannn heard the terseness in Nue's voice and thought he deserved it. He had been in the middle of going through his message box, but now he couldn't focus on a single word.

All he could think about was impending death and Nue, currently going through his clothes, probably naked. Rannn never felt so tempted before. He could have days or hours left, and all he wanted was to be with her.

Inside her.

Ravishing her. Consuming and pleasuring her until she couldn't think. Blood rushed to the flesh between his legs again.

What the *hell* was wrong with him?

Why couldn't he get her body out of his mind? He couldn't do anything with her. They had no time for him to give in. Besides, he needed to stay focused. There was no point in lusting after her.

No explanation or mental exercises lessened the desire to walk back into his cabin and claim every part of her body. And, more importantly, to be a better lover than her fingers.

No. NO.

Shaking his head, he knew he had to focus on something else. He wasn't a youth in transition. He could control himself.

His shipmates could be dying, and he was thinking about blitzing? Seth of Stars must be so disappointed.

"Chollar," he called out loud, knowing that the Master Elder Cerebral would hear him. Even though he was in a small ship five hundred miles from Garna per his agreement with the Yunkin admirals.

"Yes?"

Rannn stood up. "Can you stop these thoughts?"

"Thoughts of being with the female you want? No. Not that I can't, but because you're an idiot."

"I have a crew to protect. I need to be focused." Rannn's eyes found their way to the cabin door. His desire to have her twisted into a need to protect her.

Honor demanded that he safeguard.

"Your crew is efficient. They are doing their jobs. There is nothing more you can do."

"There is always something to do. Like getting updated on who sent the delivery pod with the biohazard."

"Sands and Lita are sure the delivery pod wasn't Federation manufactured. They also know it was programmed long before you arrived on Garna. So, they assume someone sent a message to the killer, and are looking through all communications sent from the ship. No suspects as of yet."

Rannn was pleased to know that. Yet he said, "There is still a disease on the ship, and a lot of people could be infected. Could be days or hours away from dying. Not to mention, the quantum system is down."

He also needed to start thinking about Calum. Because if this virus was deadly, then Rannn needed to try and take out the Numan before he died.

"Yon has been in contact with the other ships. No one is showing

signs of sickness. Neither are you. Ansel has been analyzing the virus, and he does not see anything in it that looks like the Eldon disease.”

“Doesn’t mean we’re safe.”

“You worry a lot about your crew. That’s a good quality in a leader. But you won’t be a leader forever.”

Rannn shook his head. “This conversation is over.” When nothing else was said, he was pleased that Chollar knew when to stop talking.

A quick, sharp pain shot up his arm, starting at the top of his hand. He rubbed out the sting, but the dull ache continued throbbing.

Why were both forearms hurting?

That made no sense.

The door to his office opened, and he turned to tell Nue that he would be working, but he stopped when he saw what she was wearing. “What did you do to my shirt?”

“Your shirts are huge, so I cut and retied the back so this one fit better. I also used a shirt to make a tie skirt because your pants will never fit me. I will buy you replacements.”

“I don’t need you to buy me clothes,” he said, observing that she wasn’t wearing a bra or panties, and her clothes were tight enough for him to notice.

Resting an arm on the top of a chair, she said, “Are you busy?”

“Yes,” he said without thinking.

She looked at the black screens. “Doing what?”

“I need to plan the next mission for finding Calum.”

“Oh, good. Do you have the coordinates to the ship? I can make a flight plan since I’m sure he’s not on any Federation routes.”

It wasn’t her job to do the flight plans. She wasn’t Federation anymore. It was on the tip of his tongue to say so, but he didn’t.

There was honor in accepting help from qualified sources. She was a quality source.

With the Minky screen to the left, he pulled up the coordinates they'd gotten from Fynbar's bot. Nue moved to his side, observed the numbers, and began tapping the screen, getting to work.

He tried not to look at her profile too long, but it was hard. She was covered, but he could see the outline of everything, and he could feel his blood begin to pulse between his legs. Again.

His fingers almost itched to touch.

Forcing his hands into fists, he lowered them under the table to thwart the temptation.

"Have you ever played pinmon?" she asked out of nowhere. "I bet you'd be a good player. You keep your expressions to a minimum."

"Is that a compliment?" he asked, not sure that he was keeping his expressions to a minimum at the moment.

The ache in his arm settled into his bone, and he clenched his teeth.

"Got the numbers," she said, typing them quickly into the nearby Minky screen.

In his seated position, he could easily picture his hands on her hips, taking her from behind. Plunging deep with all his might.

Good Seth, he felt like a youth with no control of his thoughts or manhood. He told himself to focus on what needed to be done. He didn't have time for physical indulgences. He had a mission to plan, damn it.

Pulling his eyes away from her, he blandly looked at the program.

"Do you want the fastest route, or would you like to make the attack look natural before you seize the ship?"

Good question. "Plan a natural route."

"Done," she said, turning around. "Now what? Do we head that way, or do you send a team?"

"I will wait until my team is all together and then join the mission to intercept Calum's ship."

He noticed the look of hurt in her eyes when he said *my team*. It wasn't a slight against her, it was just too dangerous to let her off the ship—out of his sight. Without apologizing, he sent the route to Yon.

Then he brought up the star map and started thinking of the best play to catch Calum unawares without causing him to unleash another disease. They needed to take him by surprise.

He figured that she would stomp out, pissed to be excluded. Instead, she sat down next to him. "Is there anything else I can do to help?"

"No, you did a good job with the route."

"How about an ice sheet, then?"

Rannn didn't know why she was talking about an ice sheet. But before he could ask, she pointed at his arm. "You keep rubbing your forearm and wrist. Ice might help."

When had he started doing that? "I'm fine."

She huffed, then stood up and walked into the other room. A second later, she walked back in, grabbed his hand, and shoved the medscope into it.

"I said, I'm fine," he gritted out.

Nue was already walking away when she said, "Whatever, Rannn."

14

NOT GIVING UP

Nue grabbed a Minky pad and walked to the bed. Powering it up, she went to the non-Federation video archives. She found a documentary of a female redecorating cabins so they felt less empty and more like home.

Settling on her stomach, she tried not to think about Rannn completely cutting her out of the mission. She shouldn't be upset, especially considering she didn't want to be a part of the crew. But still.

Also, she didn't like that Rannn was going off himself. As captain, his job was to direct, not to go and put himself in danger.

Stupid Yunkin.

Stupid *her* that she cared about someone who didn't deserve it.

"Nue," Rannn said, pulling her attention away from the screen. She didn't even know that he was inside the room.

"Yes?"

"My accounts are monitored at all times. You can't watch that on my ID."

Smashing a finger against the power button, she flipped the pad to the end of the bed. "Fine. I would have used mine, but it's unavailable, and I don't have authorization to open it up."

"I know. As mentioned, I put in a request for your Federation ID to be terminated. Especially given your choice to not remain with the crew. After your court case is over, I can put in for a non-Federation ID."

"I know how to put in a request for non-Fed ID. I'm not an idiot."

"I know you're not an idiot," he said, moving closer to the bed but not getting on it.

Skimming a finger over the blanket, she tried to think of something else to do. She couldn't just sit on the bed and do nothing. Not alone, anyway. "What about music? Is that against captain protocol?"

"No, but I don't usually listen to anything."

Too bad, Ranny-boy.

Crawling the short way to the Minky pad on her knees, she snatched it back up, powered it back on, and found her favorite upbeat music. She hit play. After the first few chords, she already felt better.

"Sounds familiar," Rannn said.

"It's about fifty years old, so that makes sense."

"What does that mean?"

She smiled. "Nothing."

His brows edged even further together. "Were you trying to make a condescending remark?"

"Not at all," she said, feeling the music. Sliding off the bed, she gave in to her impulse and swayed to the beat. "I feel like cleaning."

"That's what the duros are for," Rannn said from behind her.

The Yunkin had no idea the gift she was giving him. A Sennite female would not offer to clean another's home.

Ever.

Especially a male's abode. But she was feeling better with the music. And she liked the distraction from how sad she honestly felt about Rannn going out on a mission—without her—and possibly getting hurt.

It was like she cared. Honest to Seth, *cared* about him.

"Nue," Rannn called. She peered up at him from the kitchenette, where his food package from earlier had started to solidify.

"Yes?"

"Don't take this opportunity to snoop in my messages or my private logs."

Folding her arms over her chest, she cocked her head and pursed her lips. "Afraid I'm going to find your dirty secrets?"

He hardened his gaze as if demanding that she agree and not question.

"Is that expression supposed to scare me? It doesn't. Because worst-case scenario, you accuse me of snooping and put me in the brig. Or, you decide to ship me off to my birth planet. Or to Marnak where I grew up. Regardless, I'll deal with it and move on like I always do. But thanks for reminding me how annoyingly *Yunkin* you are."

Rannn was silent for a while. Long enough for her to grab the Minky, shut it off, and go back to the mess. She wanted to comment on the fact that he was just standing there, but the jerk was probably stewing on how blunt she'd been.

But she had to be.

He made her crazy.

Rannn grabbed the Minky pad, turned the music back on, and left the device on the table. He didn't say a word, just gave in to her music and let it be.

Why did that bother her?

Because he was being nice.

And she liked it.

Damn her stupid Terran hormones. If she were pure Sennite, she doubted she would be so damn twisted up right now. Thankfully, no one but her knew about her little flaw.

15

HELP

Rannn leaned against his Minky table, arms crossed, remembering the conversation he'd just had with Nue. He couldn't explain the radiating anger he felt at her words. Did she really think he would put her in the brig? After everything that he had done for her?

He was practically shaking with the need to take those hips she moved and hold them against his body. She had no idea that in those few seconds, he'd imagined more than a dozen ways to take her and pleasure her until she was limp.

But he didn't. Because he was honorable, and he couldn't take advantage of her.

It was wrong to invite her to blitz. What if she felt obligated?

No, she was a Sennite. She wouldn't feel obligated to do anything.

Regardless, he wasn't the male she'd alluded to earlier. He would never stoop so low as to punish her for something so trivial.

Did she really think he was that bad? Did she still hate him?

If she did, she wouldn't have danced like that in front of him.

Was she trying to trick him somehow?

Chollar answered his thoughts. *"She's not faking her interest, you idiot. I didn't tell you about the murder charges for you to clear her record and alienate her. I did it so you could do what you want to do."*

Rannn sat, not wanting to discuss his personal feelings.

"Then don't discuss, just listen. You can have her, if you choose. All you have to do is act."

He was not going to initiate an intimate relationship just because he was lusty. They could die, and he wasn't going to make his last act under Seth's universe a lusty impulse.

He had a duty to his people. And she was Sennite. They didn't marry or mate. Everyone knew that.

"Sci wants me to stop talking to you. He thinks you need to make your own choices. So, this is the last time I will help. But trust me, Rannn, she's not out to use or hurt you."

It was suddenly silent in his mind, and Rannn assumed the conversation was over. Back to his thoughts, he wondered if he should go back and talk to Nue. Except, what was there to say?

Flexing his wrist, he tried to stretch out the bone, wishing the ache would go away.

The medscope was just to his right. With Nue occupied, he reached for it and held it tightly, waiting for the machine to work.

Nothing.

He waited a little bit longer.

Still nothing.

Maybe whatever was wrong would just take a long time to heal. Drawing the medscope around his neck, he hoped the pain would go away, but he refused to dwell on it. Instead, he video-dialed Yon.

Ansel answered Yon's Minky. "Hello, Captain."

"Where's Yon?"

Ansel turned his head. "Yon, it's for you."

"Coming."

Rannn sat back and squared his shoulders, feeling the growing ache and...something else. He felt *off*. And mentally out of sorts. Angry, disappointed, and sexually deprived. Something was...wrong, and he couldn't understand what was driving his lack of control.

"Captain."

"Well?" he snapped out.

Yon narrowed his eyes for a moment and then said, "Clalls is headed to the landing ports. He will be fitted to an evo-suit and will be back on the ship shortly. Vivra and Pax have been brought on board, also in evo-suits. Chollar is ready to follow me and the transporter I will be taking to fly out on this mission. I liked your idea of faking a small engine fire in Chollar's ship so he could spin out towards Calum's. But I think we can just claim engine failure instead of a fire. Safer that way. That way, he can do a quick scan without looking like we know Calum is there, then knock him out and drag the ship back here for Ansel to take over."

"That's a good plan," Rannn said, not overly happy that Yon had thought of a better idea. Rannn was a strategist. He always came up with great plans. But then another thought came to him. "Is there a reason you didn't tell me about your amendment sooner?"

"I was going to tell you once we were in the galleon. If you had waited another ten minutes, I would have called you," Yon said without even a hint of remorse. His second in command looked off-screen again. "Ah, here they are. Time to go."

Rannn's lips pressed together. His body tensed, and he honestly didn't understand why he was so pissed off at Yon.

When Yon looked back to the screen, he tilted his head. "You have something to add?"

"No."

"Worried about the mission? Pissed at being quarantined? Or are you having issues with your cabinmate?"

All of the bloody above. And none of his damn business. "Try not to die this time. You seem to have a tendency to do that."

Yon smirked. "I don't always die. We'll be okay. I'll call you if we have any problems, but no news is good news, all right?"

"All right," Rannn said, taking control of his emotions and remembering that Yon was smart and capable. Not to mention, he was going with Pax, Vivra, Chollar, and Jandy. They would be fine. They didn't need him.

They didn't need...him.

That was what bothered him. And it shouldn't. He had planned and executed several missions where Yon and Pax had left to lead. Why did it bother him now?

More to the point, why was he getting so frustrated by it? Rannn wasn't emotional. Not like this. Everyone, including himself, knew that.

Leaving his thoughts, he focused on the screen where Ansel stood. "You seem distracted. Is something wrong?"

He shook his head.

Ansel narrowed his eyes for a second but didn't comment on his mood again. "I have something. The video just finished uploading."

"What video?" Rannn asked, getting frustrated that things were happening without his knowledge. He almost died, and everyone treated him like a journal—updating when they felt like it.

"My pods reached Cherrying a while back. I sent them while I was in the Outworlds. I figured it would be better to get a head start, so I would have the video waiting when I returned." Ansel made a face that said: *because I'm a genius.*

Ansel continued. "I've uploaded the video and began

unloading the samples in the lab that Vivra just vacated. This is Cherrying. The planet Calum used as his lab."

Rannn observed the hologram. "Looks dead."

A light smear of blue, green, and some reds didn't make any sense until the faded images became clear. Bodies. All with dead, petrified-looking expressions. The only things moving were niskies. Snake-like creatures that fed on carrion if no other food was available.

Niskies had a scathy barbist-like face and skin, but the body was thinner, and the legs were bony.

"That's a lot of niskies."

"There isn't a lab in any of the footage," Ansel said as he paused the video. My preliminary guess is that Cherrying was a dumping ground."

"Why dump them on a planet? Why not burn them or eject them into space? Calum has been on a ship for a while. It makes no sense why he would go to all the trouble to dump bodies."

Ansel's brows rose for a moment before he said, "Like I said, it's a dumping ground. And if Calum is not using it as a mass grave, he's using it as a natural breeding ground for antibodies. Those niskies are great for that. If they can eat the dead and get through the sickness, then they will have natural immunity. It was something my mother taught him."

"Is Calum looking for antibodies for himself? Wouldn't he be able to make them?"

Ansel half-smiled as if he were amused at the back and forth. "Why waste the effort doing that when the niskies can do it for him."

"Hmmm," Rannn said, leaning back. "Wait, did you happen to bring back one of those niskies? That might be a good idea in case Calum unleashes a disease."

"Of course, I did. I'm already checking the body for matches to the virus on board," Ansel said with a scowl.

Rannn felt a rise in his emotions again. Damn it. What was wrong with him? This was a good thing. His team was doing exactly as they should.

With that thought, he tapped the appliance app to his cabin and turned off the lights and his Minky pad. It was the quickest way to bring Nue to him.

It wasn't until after he had done so that he wondered why he couldn't just get up and ask her to come to his office like a normal person.

Worse, he hoped she came in a little pissed.

There was something seriously wrong with him.

Behind him, Rannn heard a very female growl. "You turned off the power?"

He held a finger to his lips. "Shhhh. Daddy's working."

What did he just say?

Nue snorted. "Tell me something I don't know." But then she walked in and stood by his side. He felt her heat against his arm. She placed a hand in front of the table and another at the back of his chair, getting in close.

He could smell her female scent, and he inhaled silently.

Good Seth of Stars, she smelled like heaven.

"This is a private call," he said in a tone that lacked heat.

Thankfully, Ansel didn't act as if he heard any of it.

"How are things coming with the Sennites? You figure it out yet?" Nue asked, ignoring him.

Ansel's lips pursed. "No. So far, all the water and air samples have come back negative."

Rannn felt his stomach clench when Nue moved herself to his lap. She couldn't be doing this... good Seth, he was already hard and practically panting. He was screwed. Having her weight on his thigh felt...right.

It felt as if she belonged there—and always had.

His hands found their way around her body, and one word penetrated his soul.

Mine.

Only mine.

Nue cleared her throat. "Have you or the doctors verified that it wasn't the males? It could be a toxin in a bad food crop."

Ansel smoothly responded, "Yes, I confirmed the males are not sterile. It's only the females, ages twelve and up. And no, it's not a crop because no single farmer feeds the entire planet."

"True. But are you sure it's all females twelve and up?"

Ansel firmly nodded.

"That's the age the females are given birth control. I don't know if you're aware, but no Sennite is allowed to give birth without consent. And the father has to be from the breeding program so his genetics are approved."

Ansel winced. "Yes, I'm aware of that barbaric law."

"I didn't bring it up to talk about the law. It's about the birth control. What if it's that?"

Ansel started to shake his head, then stopped and just stared. A second later, he said, "I've got to go."

The holographic video from the Minky table ended, and it went back to looking just like a desk.

Nue turned towards Rannn and gave him a look.

Rannn suspected that she might say something about their earlier conversation. Or even his unmistakable steely hard cock. Instead, she mock-frowned. "I think we need to talk about the alarming lack of personality in your cabin."

16

APOLOGY

Leaning back in his seat, he adjusted so he could see her clearly. And to try to give her room to talk. But something dark inside him knew...she wouldn't leave without him tasting her.

"I don't like clutter," he said as sensibly as possible.

"A few pictures on the wall is not clutter."

"I don't like pictures of other people on my walls."

"Why?" She winced.

"Makes me miss them more."

It was an honest answer, one he figured would get him a scowl. Nope. Nue pushed her lower lip out instead.

"That's cute."

It was logical.

"Would you mind if I put up a few things? I can be crafty. But I will take them down when I leave so you don't miss me, too."

"When you leave..." he repeated, not liking that she planned to leave at all.

"I'll have to leave when Ansel is done running the tests for the biohazard. I mean, I have my own room, and you clearly don't like me in your way."

"You're not in my way."

And she wasn't leaving.

Ever.

Nue nibbled her bottom lip, staring at nothing in particular. He assumed she was thinking of something as stupid as leaving, so he said, "Your cabin will have to be reassigned to another crewmember who's Federation. Which means, you will be staying with me until absolutely everything has been resolved."

"Will I be able to get my stuff?"

"Maybe," he said with a considerable amount of frustration.

Raising her brows, she said, "And how exactly can I *maybe* get my stuff?"

Honestly, there was no reason she couldn't get her stuff. But he didn't want her going alone. "We'll go after we're cleared, and when I have time to take you to get it."

Rolling her eyes, she grumbled, "Yunkins."

"You say that like you hate me and my kind." He sat up and got in her face. She sat taller, but that in no way made him feel less in control.

"I don't hate you," she said, leaning in farther, her lips practically on his. He could feel her breath as she spoke. "I just hate when Yunkins act like their word is law."

"I'm the captain. My word *is* law."

She cut her eyes to his mouth, and his heart doubled its efforts. Blood engorged his shaft. He wanted her more and more by the second.

"Is it? Or do you just like being in control?" she whispered before nipping his lip.

She'd just sealed her fate.

"Not all Yunkins are the same," he said before pulling her top lip into his mouth for a second.

"Don't care about any other Yunkins," she said slyly, moving to straddle his legs. He grabbed her ass and pulled her up and close so she could feel how much he wanted her.

"Good," he growled. "Because no other Yunkin can have you."

Her lids lowered as if just the feeling of his dick might make her come. Good Seth, he was almost shaking with need. She exhaled as she rubbed her bare sex against him, her makeshift skirt giving him easy access.

He took her neck and squeezed, getting her attention. "Nue," he growled. "You better be sure you want this? Do you understand?"

"Yes."

"No, you don't. So let me make this clear. If we do this, you're mine. Only mine."

"Yes."

"Yes, what?" he said, using his thumb to run along the seam of her sex.

"Yes, I want this."

Holding her throat, he could feel his breath shudder. "I'm not going to touch you until you tell me you want me forever. Say it."

"No one else but you."

Damn right. He pulled her down and consumed her mouth. At the same time, he kept pressure on her bundle of nerves and rubbed, giving her a double-assault she would never forget. She kissed him back, full-throttle, with whimpers and nails in his skin.

Damn, she was wild and passionate. And *his*.

Seth of Stars, was this a dream? Regardless, it was a gift. One for the taking.

Her taste became branded in his mouth. He would never want another taste, another female ever again. Nue was it for him.

Her noises peaked, and he could feel her sex begin to clench; she was coming on his hand. He continued until she was done and had pulled away from his mouth, eyes full of heat and passion.

"I want you inside me. Now," she said breathlessly.

He pushed her back, ready to unfasten his pants, ignoring the burning ache in his arms. Suddenly, Sci flashed in his mind, mouthing the word *sorry*.

Sci blinked out of existence, and more images flooded Rannn's brain. Several Yunkins—crewmembers on Garna— were in their beds, rocking back and forth in pain.

The images weren't a product of his paranoia. They were from Sci.

Rannn recognized the rooms but not all the faces. In his mind, he asked, *"Are they dying?"*

Sci appeared in his mind again, shaking his head.

Rannn asked, *"Are they in pain?"*

Sci nodded.

Just then, Rann became aware that Nue was still sitting in his lap, eyes no longer so full of lust. "Are you talking to me?"

"There's a problem on the officers' evacuation ships," he said, taking her mouth with a kiss again, though he did it more to center himself than for his wildly throbbing need. "I have to take care of this."

He watched her eyes, hoping she didn't get dramatic like his wife used to.

Nue looked at his crotch. "I'll see you later." To his face, she said, "Turn on the lights. Mommy has some redecorating to do."

Rannn didn't know why he liked it when she referred to herself as *Mommy*, but it made him think of putting a baby in her immediately. After all, she'd just agreed to be his wife.

He kissed her again, needing her taste. "You got it." Then he turned on the lights and watched her walk away.

17

RUMORS

His Minky table pinged with an incoming video call from Sands. Rannn accepted and watched as the black screen opened up to a Bolark sitting at a console inside a bridge.

"Officer Sol?" Rannn said, wondering why he'd gotten the call from Sands. Then he remembered that the quantum system was out, and Sands must have done something to keep Garna connected to their evacuated ships.

Sands was a brilliant cyborg.

"Captain." Sol cleared his throat. "Um, we might have a problem aboard."

Alarm coiled in Rannn's stomach.

Seth. No.

"What is it?" Rannn said as he leaned in slightly.

Sol winced. "I think the medscopes on board are broken."

Rannn leaned in farther. "Explain. Who's sick, and how many medscopes have you tried?"

"We have fifty medscopes on board and...thirty sick Yunkins. " He exhaled as if he were delivering the worst news possible.

"Sol, look at me," Rannn instructed. When the male did,

Rannn continued. "I can't help if I don't know what the problem is."

"All the Yunkins on board seem to be sick. We have no medical staff, so they locked themselves in their rooms. But others can hear them groaning in pain. I'm...worried for the crew."

Rannn felt Sol's fears.

In his mind, Rannn asked Sci, *"Does Ansel know about this?"*

Sci's image popped into his mind and shook his head.

That frustrated Rannn and gave him something to set his energy to in equal measure. To Sol, he said, "I'm going to talk to Ansel and discuss bringing the Yunkins back on board. Then I will check to make sure you have an abundance of working medscopes in case the others have the same problem."

"Thank you, Captain."

Rannn ended the call. He saw Nue to his right. He didn't know if he was disappointed that she was eavesdropping on his conversation, or pleased to see her, to have her back in his presence.

She pointed at his arm. "If this is only affecting Yunkins, then Calum specifically targeted your race. I don't feel any pain at all. And you haven't stopped rubbing your arms and knuckles."

He hadn't even thought about himself. But as soon as she said it, Rannn knew that she was right. He was infected. "I know. I'm about to call Ansel."

Nue crossed her arms and waited as if she didn't believe him. Or maybe she was just concerned. He wasn't sure, but he knew which one he preferred it to be.

Making a show of it, he dropped his finger to the Minky table and punched in Ansel's ID, then gave her an *are you satisfied now* look.

Nue nodded and mouthed, "Thank you," which confirmed that she cared. He liked that way too damn much.

Ansel accepted after the first ring. "Hold on," the doctor said as he held up a finger then walked off-screen.

Rannn didn't want to hold on, so he began talking anyway. "All the Yunkins on our officers' Galleon ship are reporting aching pain. And none of the medscopes are working. Officer Sol called me to tell me this. To add to that, my arms have a bone-deep ache, and the medscope I'm wearing is doing nothing."

The screen was silent for over twenty seconds. Ansel walked into camera view again with a look somewhere between irritated and perplexed. "How long have you felt this pain?"

"Since I woke up from the arsenice."

"And you didn't tell me?"

"I wouldn't have told you if the other Yunkins didn't have the same confusing pain. I'm not bleeding or dying, so it's not really worth mentioning."

Ansel's brows rose as if he were silently chastising Rannn. "Or you have a pretty cabinmate that you don't want to seem weak in front of," Ansel accused.

Rannn could feel Nue's eyes on him, but he didn't bother looking. Instead, he said, "We need to get those Yunkins back to Garna. And we need medscopes that work."

Ansel pursed his lips then reluctantly said, "Come down to medical so I can run a scan and double-check the medscope. Don't bother getting in an evo-suit, the virus is in all the vents. I have been exposed to it already, and everyone else is out of the medical bay."

Terminating the call without saying another word, Rannn gestured for Nue to follow him. However, the second they walked out of the office and into the hall, he caught the back of her tied shirt and decided to make a quick stop in her room.

Rannn didn't need anyone to see her body. That was for him only.

Rannn stood in the medscanner, watching Ansel tap the Minky screen harder than he needed to.

"Is the medscanner broken, too?"

"Nothing is broken," Ansel growled and stabbed at the screen. "See, right there." Pointing at the screen, he declared, "Your bones are fractured. That is the cause of the pain."

"Fractured?" Nue repeated, peering up with worry.

"I punched the wall outside my office," he told her, and then realized a second later that he shouldn't have.

"Why?" she asked.

He almost said, "*because I felt like it*," but chose to ignore it altogether and turn to Ansel. "But I only used my dominant hand. There is no reason for both arms to hurt."

"It's not an injury," Ansel clarified. "What I meant was, the bone fractured for some reason, and remodeling is happening. That's why you feel bone aches."

"How could my bones fracture if I didn't do anything to them?" Rannn wasn't a medical anything, but even he didn't see the logic in that assessment.

Ansel shook his head and said, "I don't know. I've never seen this before. Whatever it is, it's not natural. It was created."

"Can you predict what the virus is doing? What the end result will be?" he asked, feeling the raw ache even more. Again, he didn't know anything, so his mind worried that he was mutating or something. Maybe his bones would all break apart, and he wouldn't have arms or legs or anything anymore.

No.

He couldn't allow himself to think like that. It was too much.

Ansel peered down for a moment. "I need to get samples and run more tests."

"What tests do you need to run to find out what will happen?" Nue asked, standing next to him. Her small hands lightly touched his arm and rubbed the side as if to say that she was there for him.

Her concern was genuine, and he allowed himself to accept her touch without thinking it was a ruse.

"A lot," Ansel said, looking at the results.

"Since Calum only targeted Yunkins, do you think he was trying to send a message to the other races? Or was this because he knew I was after him?" Rannn asked.

Ansel shrugged. "I doubt he was concerned about someone like you looking for him. To him, you don't have the intelligence to catch him. But bio-hacking is old technology. I don't know if this is Calum's doing. He likes death. Though not the slow kind. This is..." He waved his hand towards the screen. "It's more like a...I don't know."

Rannn saw an image flash in his mind—Sasha docking with the Yunkins from the other ship. "Sasha's back with the others."

Ansel nodded. "Sci just told me, too."

"Is there anything I can do to help?" Nue asked.

Ansel shook his head. "No. It would be hard to explain the medical procedures to you. Just give me some time to figure this out."

Rannn looked around the medical bay, picturing how full it was about to be with the other Yunkins. Suddenly, he had a thought. Speaking aloud, he said, "What if this is something that not only we are suffering from?"

Ansel's mouth dropped as if he were about to say something, but Rannn added, "What if this virus is also on Yunkin, and some idiot shut down the quantum network to stop all long-distance pod deliveries?"

Nue stepped in front of him and touched his chest. "It seems to be a recent thing for our ship. But what if it hit other ships, too. Before it hit here. Do you know any other Yunkin captains?"

Did he know any other Yunkin captains? Did he bleed grey? "Yes," he said and walked to the Minky screen, scrolling to the first captain he knew. He hit transmit. The call didn't go through.

Rannn frowned at the network error. He sent a message to Sands with a Federation ID he wanted to get ahold of.

A moment later, the screen became outlined in blue, indicating that a call was being initiated. Three rings later, it was answered.

The other side of the video call was a dark screen, but Rannn could tell it wasn't an issue with the transmission. It was a dark room.

"Who are you?"

Rannn didn't recognize the voice. "Captain Adroon?"

"Adroon is dead. Was shot with something from a delivery pod, threw up for several minutes, and then died of suffocation. Who are you, and how did you get into my ship's system?"

Rannn knew the voice of a scared Yunkin who was forced to take command during a chaotic event. He'd been there once, too. But he wasn't about to cut the Yunkin any slack. "My name is Captain Rannn. My engineer has special skills in communication. But I'm calling because I believe a bio-focused disease is affecting all Yunkins. I was calling to see if your crew might have similar, bone-deep aches."

Rannn heard the male grunt as if he were sitting up. A second later, a light illuminated the screen, and it took all his training not to respond.

Nue gasped as she clutched his shirt.

On the other side of the screen was a pale-skinned male with long, Yunkin hair and Night Demon horns protruding out of his forehead. The stranger rubbed the base of his forehead before looking into the screen. "Yeah, we had the aches. And then these things popped out of my skull." He pointed at his head. "It's interesting that you have the aches but have not turned into this...atrocity yet."

Rannn looked to Ansel for a second and then told the male, "Everyone on board has horns?"

"No, just the Yunkins. No one else was cursed," he sneered.

Rannn scanned the room and found Ansel staring at the screen.

"It spread through my ship in less than a few hours." The male looked at his hand. "Whatever this is, it affected more than just my body. I've never been angrier in my life. I want to find out who did this and rip them apart with my bare hands. I want to *drink their blood.*"

Rannn had felt that angry when he was on Angny. Had remembered feeling the need for vengeance. But he would never have confessed it. Things like drinking a dead man's blood went too far, even for revenge.

"The need for payback is natural," Rannn said, hoping to remind the male that he wasn't lost. He was just...deformed.

"Rannn, was it?" The male stared at the screen in a predatory way. "I heard a rumor that you have an Outworlder on your ship? And a Numan doctor, too. Is that true?"

"It's true. What of it?"

A look of disappointment spread over the male's face. "So, this could be because of you. Your Numan doctor had access to Federation transports."

Beside him, Nue hissed. "Oh, he did not..."

Rannn grabbed her hand and squeezed, a command to let him handle this. "I understand being upset at the person who did this. But to blame me or anyone from my crew without evidence is *not* the Federation way. Get control of yourself, boy."

Leaning in, the mutant Yunkin said, "Only a Numan could

do this. And, yes, I blame you for letting that predator into our ranks. You can be sure I will find you as soon as the network is back up."

Nue's nails dug into his skin. Oddly enough, it was both flattering and soothing to his ego.

"You do realize I am the captain of Garna, the star carrier?"

"I don't care what ship you're on. I will find you and kill you."

Rannn folded his arms over his chest. Maybe he was wrong to think the disease only affected the person's body. Perhaps it also skewed a person's rational thinking. "Greater opponents have tried to kill me and failed."

"I won't fail," the mutant said, smashing his horns into the screen and breaking the image.

Rannn ended the call. As soon as he did, Nue cursed the Yunkin in every colorful way a female could.

Just then, Sci walked in with his hands in the air as if holding up all the floating Yunkins on an invisible platter. Each one writhed in pain.

Nue cursed again, and Rannn placed a finger over her lips. "As much as I appreciate you defending me, we need to think about the crew first. Hold it together."

"That Yunkin-whatever was wrong. How can you not be pissed?" she asked with a frown.

"Easy. I have other things to worry about."

"Rannn," Sci called from the other side of the room. Ansel was there, rubbing his head, and Rannn worried for the first time that Ansel might be overloaded.

Nue grabbed his hand and whispered, "Ansel looks...frazzled."

Rannn snorted at her term, but he couldn't think of a better one. Walking hand-in-hand, he didn't even care if the others saw. He didn't even try to hide it. They would have figured it out sooner or later anyway.

In a corner, Ansel said, "The medscopes must have slowed the progression of the virus. I have to figure out what is causing the remodeling and stop it."

Nue was the first to ask, "Does that mean the medscopes will fail eventually?"

Ansel's nostrils flared. "Yes."

Sci gave him a quick look that conveyed a lot. Rannn took Sci's mental concerns and voiced them. "You have too much going on. You need help."

"I don't need help," Ansel shot back. "And even if I did, no one can help."

"Why can't we?" Nue asked.

"Because it would take too long to explain what needs to be done," Ansel clarified, then cut his eyes to Sci. "No....I can do this... No..... Also, no..... Are you serious?"

Nue looked up at him and slanted her eyes in Sci's direction. Rannn shrugged, letting her know that he had no idea what kind of unspoken fight Sci was currently having with Ansel.

Ansel leaned his head back stiffly, then a second later, all that stiffness was gone. "Oh, that makes sense. Fine. Okay."

Sci nodded before turning around and announcing, "I will be back soon."

"If he wants money, tell him I saved his life, and he owes me," Ansel shouted at Sci, who smiled with an evil little crook to his mouth.

"I won't let him say no."

Ansel nodded.

Once Sci had left, Rannn demanded, "Want to fill me in?" Because he was tired of being the last to know. He was the captain, wasn't he?

"Sci suggested picking up my brother, Penner."

"You have a brother?" Nue said like the idea of Numans being biological creatures was preposterous.

Ansel eyed her. "Penner is a microbiology expert. Calum, his clone, was created from his DNA. If anyone can work on the Sennite problem while I work on your issue, it's him."

There was the Ansel Rannn knew. Brilliant with unwavering confidence. Rannn almost smiled at him for not admitting that he needed Penner's help. He was delegating the easy work.

"Come. Take a seat so I can biopsy the bone and see what I'm dealing with," Ansel said to Rannn as he pointed at an empty chair.

18

YUNKINS AROUND THE GALAXY

Rannn wanted to go back to his office alone to scream. The pain was growing, and nothing aside from being knocked out had helped his crewmates—male or female. But he remained in medical, watching and waiting as Ansel flitted between the Yunkin crewmates and his lab.

Nue had not left his side, sitting in a visitor's chair. He felt like a skem, wishing she would leave so he didn't have to hold back his responses to the pain. But imagining her alone without him unsettled him, as well.

He held the medscope as tightly as he could, his hand in his pocket, worried about what he would look like with Night Demon attributes. Not that he was vain, but the mutation was an act of war against his people.

Rannn couldn't help but think that this was all Calum's doing. He hoped that Yon soon found the bastard and could get the antidote to cure his crew and the others affected.

His Minky pad pinged with a call. It hurt like the mother of Seth as he pulled it out, rested the pad on his thigh, and hit accept.

"Clalls," he gritted out.

"Captain, I'm headed back to the ship. But before I connect this call, I just want to reiterate our deal."

Rannn could feel his lip curl up. "There was no deal. There was only my order."

Clalls inhaled loudly. "You said you'd think about it."

"I will think about killing you if you don't tell me what information you have."

"Right, well, you sound like you're in the perfect mood to take this call. Hopefully, you're alone."

Rannn would have liked to be alone. But knowing that the call would be sensitive, it was honorable to stay so everyone could hear. It was the right thing to do.

Nue slightly tilted her head as if she were interested in the call but tried to make it less obvious. He didn't comment on it because he looked over to Ansel and jerked his chin towards the screen. Ansel should hear this.

"I don't keep secrets, Demon. Just put the call through."

"Captain, I respect that about you. But this *will* be hard for you."

Rannn understood what Clalls was referring to. What'd happened to Adroon's crew must have happened on his home planet, as well. "If you're referring to the mutation, Yunkins turning into Night Demons, I already know."

"You do?"

"I damn well can feel the change happening to me, and I'm not freaking out. Now stop being a tarq and put my *mother on the bloody line!*"

"Okay. I, ah, didn't know you were turning into a mutation. Does Ansel know about this? Can't he fix it?" Clalls' tone conveyed more concern than interest.

"CLALLS," Rannn bellowed in warning.

"All right, all right, here's your mum."

A quick ping sounded, and then he heard a familiar, "Hello?"

"Mother, are you all right?"

"Rannn? Oh, sweetie. How...you know what? I don't even care how you found a Rana to break into my house to give me this hacked Minky pad."

Rannn looked at Nue when his mother referred to a Rana breaking into his mother's house. Surely, his mother was wrong.

No way would Clalls send a Rana to Yunkin.

But then, that sounded like a very Clalls thing to do.

Looking at Ansel, the Numan just shrugged as if to say: *the Demon has skills.*

His mother continued. "She is very polite, by the way. Nova, you said your name was?" she said to someone.

Rannn watched Nue cover her mouth. Rannn knew the name as the person who'd killed the innocent male and stole his money. The fact that Nue looked worried said that she knew her and that...was something they were going to talk about later.

On the call, they heard a female say, "Yes, ma'am."

"Rannn. She attacked the guards outside my house. I hope you can do something about that so she doesn't get in trouble. They were rather rude."

"They were threatening you, ma'am. They deserved more than what I did to them. But more importantly, this is about your son. You have five minutes to talk, then I have to get back off the planet before anyone finds my ship," Nova said, and Rannn didn't know where to begin with his questions.

There were guards outside his mother's house? They had been threatening her? What the hell was happening on his home planet?

"Nova?" Nue whispered as she leaned down to his lap. "Is that really you?"

"Nue? Why are you next to the captain? Aren't you supposed to be...I don't know, not near him?"

He could tell that Nue was going to explain, but he had five minutes, and he needed answers. He also didn't like Nue talking to a contract killer. Call him crazy, but his wife was not going to have that kind of connection.

Also, Nue was safe *next to him*, not far away from him.

A strange thought entered his mind. What if Nova tried to steal Nue away from him?

A flare of possessiveness gripped him. Which, in turn, made him grab Nue's hand and hold it. She was *his*. No one needed to worry about her. It was his responsibility to take care of her. To protect her. Even from old acquaintances who were somehow linked to Nue's file...

Oh.

Wait.

If they were linked without an eye witness—and there wasn't, he checked—it was because of blood analysis. Which meant...Nue and Nova were related.

Holy Seth.

Holy...

"Rannn, do not come back to the planet. It's not safe right now."

His mother's words ripped him out of his very unwelcome realization. It took all his self-control not to corner Nue right then and have her explain why the hell she kept that to herself. She may not have directly lied. But keeping it from him was just as bad.

"Mother, tell me everything that has happened. When did the disease hit? How many did it infect? Why have they closed down all communication?"

His mother took another long breath. "The head of the admirals council was shot with a delivery pod. He died from arsenice a few minutes later. That was days ago. Then, everyone started to feel pain in their body. Not everyone suffered in the same areas. Those who had medscopes are still in pain but not...

deformed. It was awful. There was so much agony. I refused to use a medscope. About a day ago, they popped out of my shoulders. Small, pointed bones. But at least the intense pain is gone. All my shirts are ruined now, but we don't need to talk about that."

Rannn watched as Nue covered her mouth in shock.

He felt the same.

"As soon as that started happening, everything went to hell. The quantum network was blown up. Federation security locked everyone inside, including the council admirals. Orin was able to send an escort to check on me. He said that he and his wife have horns. He told me to stay inside, not to go out until they find out who is attacking us. I have not heard from him since."

Rannn didn't like the sound of any of that. "Someone blew up the quantum network?"

Nova, the Rana who broke into his mother's house, called out, "Captain, I think you should know that all the guards I saw weren't Yunkins. They were Bolarks."

Rannn felt a coldness in his blood. Bolarks? "Any other race aside from Bolarks?"

"Nope. And you have one more minute," Nova said promptly.

"Rannn? Have you been affected?"

"Yes," Rannn said, answering his mother's question.

"Oh, I thought Ansel would have found a cure for you. He's so smart."

He caught the scowl on Ansel's face. Rannn didn't know if that was because Ansel felt bad about not knowing how to fix the issue, or because he was just being the annoying, bitter Numan he always was when Sci wasn't around.

Rannn knew the doctor was not right in the head. He had lots of bad memories that Sci kept at bay. When Sci left, Ansel didn't do so well.

Rannn decided that he would have to stay in medical until Sci returned. Ansel was too important. He couldn't leave his fate up to mental strength.

"I'm not Seth of Stars, I can't fix everything with a flick of a microscope," Ansel mumbled to himself.

"Is that Ansel I hear? Ansel, have you narrowed down what caused this?"

Ansel turned and walked away. Rannn figured that meant he was not going to openly admit to Rannn's mother that he had no clue. Rannn knew how much his mother liked Ansel. She was the one who'd asked Rannn to take Ansel after his academy graduation. She was sure that Ansel would be locked in a think tank and never let out if Rannn didn't.

Considering how hard it had been to get the Numan off the Yunkin planet, Rannn knew his mother was right. And Ansel knew it, too.

Rannn didn't think Ansel was sentimental, but he wondered if maybe, just maybe, he was ashamed that he hadn't figured it out yet.

"He's working on it, Mom. Thankfully, it's not something that is killing us off in mass numbers."

"Why would you say something like that? That's awful," his mother hissed.

"All right, times up. I have to go. Say goodbye to your son," Nova said over the call.

"Bye, Rannn. Please stay safe."

Rannn didn't get a chance to reply to that comment.

He wanted to pick up the Minky and throw it, but Clalls' voice stopped him.

"Hey, Cap, I don't know if this helps, but I don't feel any differently, and I'm part Yunkin."

"That's good to know. I'll relay that to Ansel."

"Never been so pleased to be a Night Demon already," Clalls

said, and Rannn didn't bother saying goodbye. Terminating the call, Rannn immediately found and selected Yon's ID. He needed to check on Yon. Because if this was Calum's doing, the Numan might have more diseases at the ready. Unfortunately, Yon didn't answer his call.

Rannn called again.

Nothing.

Again.

Nothing.

Then a message came from Yon: *I'm busy.*

Just then, the door to Ansel's lab opened, and the Numan walked out. Rannn grabbed his Minky, trying to stuff it back into his pocket, but his fingers trembled, and the device fell between his legs.

He cursed and hated how quickly Nue snatched it off the floor and offered it to him. He took it again, feeling the same shake. And again...the crash.

"I'll just hold it," she said without looking at him.

Rannn forced his body to stand despite the agony in his upper limbs. "Fine. Just don't..." he said with a snarl.

Nue cut her eyes to him.

Even in pain, Rannn was able to understand the threat. Or more to the point, the warning that *he* was about to cross a line. "Thank you," he said, properly chastised.

Nue tried not to be pissed off at Rannn, but the Yunkin made it impossible to see why he was being so incredibly jerkish. Seriously, why was he snapping at everyone?

Nue had so many questions. Like how in the hell did Nova end up working for Clalls?

In addition to being upset, Nue hated seeing Rannn in pain. Why wasn't he asking for pain meds?

Why were males so damn stubborn?

The rest of his Yunkin crewmates were out, and she could almost see why he would want to stay conscious, but there were things he could take that would numb his body and not his mind. Not all of them legal, but still. There was no reason he should suffer.

"Do you think Ansel would work better without an audience?" she asked, hoping he wouldn't see through her intentions.

"Ansel is not affected by people watching him. He's endured professors and the like hovering over him, questioning everything he did. He could care less. But I'm not leaving him."

Nue wondered if Rannn wanted to stay so he could be there when Ansel found the cure. Or if he simply didn't want to go back to his cabin—with her. "If Ansel won't do better or worse with you here, why not go back to your office where you can, relax? Take a pain reducer."

"I'm fine."

Okay. Gentle pushes clearly weren't going to work. "I'm not. And watching you suffer is making me crazy."

"You're welcome to leave," he said through his teeth, and she wanted to slap him right then and there. The jerk had no idea what gifts she had given him.

She cared about him.

She'd let him touch her, kiss her and get words from her she'd never told another person.

She cleaned his room and planned to decorate it to fit *him.*

Stupid, stupid male. Did he not care that she was hurting for him? That's when she felt the heat rise to her cheeks. She was embarrassed because she clearly liked him more than he did her.

How that had happened, she didn't know. And she didn't care. Because as of right now, she saw things clearly. "Fine, I'll just stop by your room and pick up the bottle of Jubriaan to clear my head since you won't be needing it."

Nue didn't bother to wait for his reply. She was done. Screw him.

Nue took a right out of medical and took the stairs, racing as fast as she could because it was the only thing she could think of that would burn out her frustrations. Like why she was wasting her time.

Eventually, Ansel would find a cure for the Yunkin and Sennite problems. Both of which she couldn't do anything to help with—because she wasn't smart enough, at least according to Ansel.

Once they were resolved, the Federation would go back to normal. She would be leaving the ship anyway. Bound to a planet where she could find a job and start over.

And forget all of this.

She reached the captain's level with her calves burning and her lungs sucking in as much air as they could get. The door to Rannn's room was closed, but his office was open. Using the connecting door at the back of the office, she strode in, ready to go straight to the kitchenette. But she stopped short.

"What are you doing in here? I thought you were staying in medical."

"Clalls is watching Ansel for me," Rannn said, pulling out both bottles from his chiller.

So, Rannn wanted to be there when the cure came in. That's why he hadn't wanted to leave. Made sense. But if he cared so much about the cure, why was he here?

"You came to stop me from touching *your* stuff?"

He glanced back, and she couldn't explain why his anger looked so damn sexy on him as if she'd just offended him. "As if I'd let you drink alone."

Was that a Yunkin slight towards females who drank? Or was he being...nice?

Rannn's hands were shaking with both bottles, and she wanted to take them, but having been around the Yunkin long enough, she knew how he got. She didn't want to emasculate him. When he got the bottles to the table, she saw his jaw clench. Poor thing was hurting but fighting with every ounce of will he had. And damn if that wasn't doing a number on her lady parts.

He wasn't angry about her drinking. He was upset that she had planned to do it alone. That had to be it. But it didn't stop her from asking, "Were you looking for an excuse to drink? Or are you here to be the less-drunk friend?"

Rannn sat down and took the bottle, shaking as he poured. "Who is Nova to you?"

He pushed the half-filled glass towards her and dumped another shaky pour.

Nue took the glass but didn't drink the liquor. She had been wrong. He wasn't here to watch over her, he was here to get answers. How classically Rannn.

Disappointed didn't even begin to explain her feelings. "She's my twin sister. And yes, she's a Rana. No, I don't know how she knows Clalls or how to contact her. She rarely contacts me, and I like it that way."

Nue picked up the glass and headed for the door. "I've told you all I know, and I'm ready to drink this and lay down. This interrogation game is getting old. I'm sure you have loads of work to do, so I'm headed back to my room. Where I'll be staying until I get a ride off this scrap piece."

She heard the crash of glass, and then a hand grabbed the waistband of her pants. Rannn tugged her to a stop, his energy radiating over her back. His mouth lowered to her ear as he spoke.

"You can get mad all you want, but you don't get to leave. You agreed to be mine, and there is no going back on your word. And I was not interrogating you. You will never see that side of me. I was asking about Nova because I don't like you keeping secrets from me. When I told you what you were accused of, you didn't bother voicing the truth. But when I told you Nova was responsible, you didn't say a word. That's not okay. Secrets aren't going to be a thing between us. Ever."

A part of Nue wanted to say there was no *them*, but the way he held her and spoke about them being a couple made all the female parts of her happy. She wasn't the only one who cared, who wanted this to work.

Knowing that helped. A lot.

"If I had told you that I know Nova, especially back then, can you honestly say you wouldn't have thought I was an accomplice?"

"No, I wouldn't have. Because by the time I learned the name, I knew the truth."

Oh, yeah. Timelines were hard to keep straight.

"Are you going to tell Clalls to help catch her so she serves her time in Debsa?" Nue didn't know why she asked. She knew what the answer would be, and she also knew that she wasn't going to like it.

"Clalls wouldn't give up his informant. Even to a captain."

Was that his way of saying no?

Nue almost smiled at that. If he was willing to not look for Nova, then maybe he wouldn't be upset about Nue's actual felony. But she couldn't get the words out of her mouth. Would he lose it and throw her in a transporter with the autopilot set to Debsa?

His Yunkin honor wouldn't let him *not* do that.

The law was the law.

"This is what's going to happen, Nue. You're going to set down that glass and crawl on my bed. I'm going to strip you, taste you, and fill you until I mark you—brand myself there. You are mine. All mine. Forever. Do you understand?"

She swallowed. "I don't want to be your forever mistress."

Turning around, she leaned back to get a good look at him. "You and I both know that Yunkins marry other Yunkins."

His blue eyes were so dark, she couldn't even see the lightness of them. All she saw was his stark desire and internal struggle. It was intoxicating. She was absolutely mesmerized by the depth of his gaze.

But he had to understand that she wasn't an idiot. And she was better than a bedpet.

"As captain of the Garna, I take you as my wife. My word is law."

Nue felt her channel clench deep in her womb. Good Seth, was he serious? "All purchases final? No returns?"

His head was already lowering. "You're mine, Nue. As captain, I have the authority to say so. As soon as you agree, anyway."

She hesitated on purpose. "Do I look like a wife? Or do I need to grow my hair out?"

"Yes, or no?" he growled.

"Mmmmm. I don't know if you're prepared for a wife like me. I'm probably going to do things you don't like, such as redecorate this empty cabin."

"Yes...or no?"

"Yes."

"No going back on your word, Nue. You accepted me, you agreed to be my wife. Now, stop playing and give me that mouth. I need it."

Giving him what he wanted, they fell back onto his bed. She backed up until he was fully on top of her, giving her his weight and sending her nerves into overdrive.

Rannn pulled back to breathe and rest his head against hers. "I've always dreamed of choosing my wife. Though I've never wanted anyone as much as I want you."

She was about to tell him to skip explanations, but she noticed that he was moving slowly. And shaking. He was using words to buy time. His arms must still be hurting.

But he didn't want her to know. Otherwise, why do *this* now?

Playing along, she said, "I've always dreamed of a husband who pleasured me to the point of losing consciousness."

Sitting back, he said, "Noted."

It sounded like he'd just accepted some challenge. She didn't think there was such a thing as having sex until she passed out, so she started laughing.

Nue had never laughed while having sex before. It was a new experience, and she couldn't say that it was a bad thing.

She removed her shirt, pushed him to his back, and crawled onto his lap.

Rannn's chest inflated as his erection pushed against his pants. She nudged the bulge with her covered sex. Leaning down, she whispered at cock-level, "Don't worry, I'll rescue you, big guy."

Unfastening his fly, she bit her lip provocatively when the grey member popped out. Wrapping a hand around his shaft, not bothering with any niceties, she stroked him, loving the silky feel. She wanted him, and she wanted him now.

Rannn hissed as he sat up. "If I wanted your hand, I would tell you."

Nue let him go, leaned back, and removed the rest of her clothes. She pushed Rannn onto his back. "I need to play with your body. So, just lay back and stay hard for me."

She wasn't really particular *how* she climaxed, as long as it was good. And Rannn looked as if he were ready to give it to her good. But this was the first time she was having sex with her husband. She planned to make it unforgettable.

"Nue, you're going to learn this fast. I control your pleasure. So be a good Mommy and give me a taste of what's mine."

Damn.

That was hot.

Taking a finger, she pushed it between her folds and into her channel then rubbed it around until she knew it was good and wet. She withdrew the digit and tapped Rannn's lower lip.

With one hand, she grabbed his hardness again. She slid the finger of her other in between his lips. The suction in his mouth as he cleaned her was divine. "Want more?"

His nostrils flared, and he nodded. "Climb up on my face and give me full access."

Oh, my.

She could feel a slight blush. She had never been directed like this before, and she couldn't say it was a bad thing.

Nue crawled up, opened her legs wide, and sat low enough to feel the wet tip of his tongue. At first, it was only light licks. She was about to change positions because it seemed like Rannn didn't know how to give proper oral, but then both hands grabbed her thighs and gripped.

Nue felt instant pricks of pain. Using the wall to keep her steady, she peered down and saw that spikes had punctured all over Rannn's forearms.

Holy Seth.

She opened her mouth to say something but hissed just as Rannn sucked her tight little bud into his mouth. The pleasure-pain combination was enough to make her lose herself.

Holding the wall, she closed her eyes and let it happen.

"Rannn," she whimpered. Holy hell, that felt so good.

He growled and dug in, devouring her, giving her sweet spot so much attention she felt the burn of a hard climax barreling down, claiming her faster than she wanted. It broke in her womb and was so raw, it was like nothing she had ever felt before.

She screamed.

Rannn didn't stop or even act as if he'd felt her come on his mouth.

She tried to lift up when the spasms calmed, but he growled for her to return. So, she stayed until he drove out another release. This time, she couldn't stand it. Clawing the wall, she burned for him and screamed his name. Her insides and thighs throbbed and squeezed as everything inside her burst with white-hot pleasure. It was the hottest thing she'd ever felt.

After the second time, she was ravenous for more—more of him filling her. She didn't care that he protested as she moved down to his sex. She took hold of him at the root and squeezed, hard. Rannn's chest rumbled.

"You need to be inside of me," she told him.

But she didn't do anything more. Simply waited for him to agree.

His nostrils flared. "You want me, you take me in one move. No going slow. You slam down on that dick, and you take me whole."

Good Seth, she might come from just listening to him talk about what she had to do. Positioning herself above him, she held his eyes and felt the head of his length at her entrance.

"All the way, Nue. I need you to take it all the way to the root."

"It's been a while," she said, just in case she failed.

"Now," he said. She dropped down, forcing past the stretching pain. It hurt. It did. He was thick, and she was tight.

She heard him call her name, but she could only focus on moving down.

Sharp pinpricks attacked her thighs. She both hated and loved the feeling.

His eyes were pitch-black, no blue at all. Both hands grabbed her hips. Rannn thrust up the remaining distance, and she screamed.

He flipped her over, bit down on her lip, and hammered inside of her, without any grace. He took. He claimed. And she accepted all of it.

Over and over, she screamed. Yes!

She could feel the thorns of the spikes on her thigh on the other. It was so much sensation she was mad with pleasure and pain.

Rannn dominated her channel, slipping in and out of her

wetness as if he owned it. As if he had known her for years. It was passion unlike anything she'd thought a Yunkin could feel. Good Seth, she never wanted it to end.

Another climax was building fast. She called out to Rannn, digging her nails into his flesh. He growled like a beast.

Her beast.

It spiraled up just as raw and hard as before, and she chanted, "Yes. Yes, yes, yes, yesssssss. RANNN."

She crashed over, falling into a bed of sparkling pleasure. Rannn thrust two more times and then sank deep. His mouth over hers, crushing her lips with a kiss.

She felt him release inside, filling the most feminine part of her body.

Rannn's kiss softened and smoothed. Then he lifted his head, breathing heavily. His expression was almost surprise mixed with relief. When he didn't look away, she felt herself blush.

Rannn kissed her lips again before sitting all the way up. Then she watched his expression fall.

"Nue," he said, looking devastated. He must have just noticed her blood and the black bones sticking out of his knuckles and forearms. Holding them up in the air, he backed off the bed. He shook his head twice and cussed at himself. "Don't move. I'm getting my medscope."

His medscope?

It couldn't have been...she looked at the smears of her yellow blood all over her body. Some were puncture wounds and other scratches. Oh wow, she hadn't thought it was that bad, but it looked terrible. Her skin was a little raw, but it looked worse than it felt. Still high from her three amazing orgasms, she genuinely didn't feel any pain.

When Rannn didn't return after a few seconds, she decided

to take a shower and clean up. Because she was not a child, she could clean her own wounds.

INSIDE THE SHOWER, her hair full of suds, the door opened. Rannn's voice carried over the water. "I told you to stay in bed. We aren't done."

"Sorry, Mommy only listens when she's getting orgasms."

The door crashed open, and Rannn stood there in a pair of Federation pants, unfastened. Nothing else. She liked the look on him.

He took her hand and pressed a medscope into it. Taking the device, she leaned her head back and used her free hand to rinse out her hair.

When she finished, she looked for any unhealed scratches and found none. Rannn was still standing there with an unemotional mask, but his arms were still covered in thick spikes. She set the device on a wall lip and applied the conditioner.

She made sure to show him, rather than speak, how much she liked that he was watching.

But when he stepped inside, she had to laugh because Rannn's pants were tented, and his arms bristled with even more black, thorn-like bones. How fascinating.

LIMP, well-pleasured, and just waking up, Nue lay naked and curled up against Rannn.

His heartbeat was slow and steady. He was still sleeping. The methodic bump, bump, bump lulled her back to that dream world, but she fought it because she wanted to take the time to enjoy Rannn when he was like this.

There was something so...innocent about his sleeping face. Nue didn't spend time with her bed partners after she took her pleasure. She was glad of it because she wanted Rannn to be the only one.

Also, she thought it was interesting that Rannn's bones only protruded when he was aroused. It was the most Night Demon thing she could imagine. And, to be honest, she wasn't upset with the added character flaw.

Was it normal to feel so content?

If so, being married would be good for her.

It had been a while since they had showered. Rannn had tried to be careful not to hurt her, but he was still getting used to the bone protrusions. But control was beyond both of them, and all they did was reach for new levels of gratification.

Rannn was no longer wincing, and he used his hand freely, so she assumed the worst of the pain was past. Which was good, because seeing Rannn hurting had not been fun.

Rannn took the hand that rested on his chest, kissed it, and then pressed it back down, covering it with his own. "Nue, I have to go back down to medical."

Oh?

Sitting up, she asked, "Are you in pain?"

He seemed okay, especially with his arms back to normal. "I'm great. But Sci just got back with Ansel's brother, and I wanted to be there."

Oh. "Can I come?"

Rannn sat up, keeping hold of her hand. "Yes..."

She raised her eyebrows because it sounded like he had more to say.

"I need to be able to focus on the mission. I have things to take care of. So, if I don't give you my full attention, you have to be okay with that."

What an adorable thing to say. He thought she was going to

be one of *those* females. Being married for a few hours wasn't going to change her basic personality. Instead of reminding him that he'd married a Sennite, she said, "I'll be okay with that as long as you're okay with me voicing my opinion."

He hesitated. "Will you expect me and everyone to follow these opinions? Because if so, I need to let you know that's not how this works. You are my wife, not my co-captain."

That was *not* an adorable thing to say.

"I understand."

"Good," he said without looking at her. He moved off the bed and grabbed his pants, but she wasn't done with the conversation.

"Just one more question," she said, grabbing her panties and pulling them on. She waited until Rannn gave her his attention. He looked leery, and he should be.

"Will you expect me to treat you like my captain? Because if so, that's not how this is going to work."

Rannn grabbed his shirt and pulled it on, not saying anything. In fact, he didn't say anything until he was fully clothed. Then, all he said was, "I'll meet you in my office when you're done getting dressed."

Nue watched the office door shut. There was a coldness to her irritation, and it was an emotion she recognized well. Self-doubt. Did she just make a life-altering mistake?

20

PENNER

Nue had been quiet since they talked, and it bothered him that she was stewing. He tried not to think about their newlywed fight. But he couldn't help it.

Was it too much to ask to have a proper wedding day where there were no fights?

For the fifth time, Rannn found himself glancing at Nue, who was petting the niskie Ansel had caught. Even though it was collared, he didn't like the snake-like dog around his wife. Those creatures ate flesh.

"Orna won't hurt her," Ansel said.

Orna? "You named it?"

"Named *her*. Of course. It's what people do when they get a pet...at least, I think."

Rannn worried that he'd left Ansel alone too long. "I thought he ate diseases and stuff. Is it even safe for that thing to be out of its lab?"

"*She* is not sick and has nothing that can transfer to you or anyone else on the ship. And leaving her in the lab isolated would be torturous for the animal. They are social creatures."

Uh...okay. "But how do you know it's safe?"

Ansel peered over at Clalls, who was on the other side of the room. The Demon was opening and closing a medbed, mumbling something about being bored. Ansel told Rannn, "The niskie has yet to eat Clalls, so I figure the pet is safe enough."

Rannn was speechless. That was Ansel's bar?

Glaring at the Demon, Ansel said, "You're going to break it. Stop."

Clalls didn't. "You took away my markers. Give 'em back, and I will."

"You were drawing on their faces."

Clalls turned to Ansel. "I was exploring my artistic talents. You're disrupting my true calling in this life."

Ansel glared ferociously. "I should have knocked the Demon out just to see if that was enough for the niskie to take a nibble."

Okay, Rannn decided, Ansel needed Sci's peaceful influence immediately.

Clalls removed his finger from the medbed. "Fine. But you owe me a set of markers, and I get to name the snake on four legs."

"She's not a snake. And her name is Orna."

Clalls rolled his eyes. "Sounds orna-narily stupid."

Ansel hissed and stomped back to the other side of medical where his microscope was. Clalls simply smiled and yelled out, "She looks more like a Nika."

Rannn didn't know why Clalls' action didn't come across as clearly before. But he was a damn clever Demon. Ansel was suicidal and grouchy. Without Sci, he was less motivated to even speak.

But seeing Ansel right now, Rannn saw he burned with motivation. Even if it was...to have his new pet eat Clalls.

Clalls was one smart Demon.

Minutes later, the medical door slid back, and Sci walked in next to Sasha, who held their baby. Behind Sci was another male in an expensive suit. He didn't look at all like Ansel. There was an air of arrogance about him, evident in his walk and the way he held himself. Until he noticed the niskie.

"What the hell?"

Rannn looked at Ansel to see if he was pleased to see his brother.

Ansel wasn't looking at Penner. Instead, he tapped on a screen with complete interest. Almost as if he were purposely avoiding his guest. Hmmm. Looked like Ansel was in a foul mood regardless if Sci was around or not.

Interesting.

"Why is there a niskie on the ship?" Penner asked, looking at Sci.

Sci was quiet for a minute and then said, "Orna is kind of like a lab pet in training."

Penner shook his head as if he were amazed at the audacity. "You mean Ansel uses him to test his experiments? I didn't think the Federation went for that kind of thing."

Rannn spoke up. "She's not being used to test experiments. It's a pet." Speaking louder so Ansel heard, he said, "One who needs proper training."

The pet with yellow eyes turned and faced Rannn but only glanced his way. Then, the niskie turned to Penner and, oddly enough, hissed.

Penner touched his chest and stepped back. "That thing belongs in a cage."

Ansel, who had been avoiding everyone, turned and smirked at the pet. Rannn wasn't sure, but he thought the doctor might have murmured, "Good girl."

"Captain." Sci cleared his throat. "This is Penner. Ansel's brother."

Penner nodded in greeting. "Captain Rannn. I had the pleasure of reading the archives regarding your career... Quite the story."

Rannn could hear the amusement in Penner's voice. Being raised around arrogant pricks like him, Rannn let the *story* comment slide. Plus, there was no reason for power games. Rannn was in command of the biggest ship in the galaxy, one with the most skilled crew.

No one could beat him.

"Penner," he said in his captain's voice. "I assume you've been updated on the issues?"

"No," Penner said with an undertone of, *and I'm not here because I want to be.*

"You're here to figure out how and why the entire Sennite planet has been sterilized," said Ansel, moving over to the other side of his counter to grab a Minky pad. He quickly typed something and then walked over, making a point to pat Orna on the head as he passed. Orna's long snake tongue slithered out to lick Ansel's hand.

Gross.

When Ansel was finished, he handed over the Minky. "Review this and figure it out. I have other things to work on."

Penner didn't look at the screen. He watched Ansel with minimal interest. "What could be more important than finding out why an entire race has been sterilized? You're a Federation medical officer. Surely, this registers as something profound."

Ansel didn't say a word, he just went back to his side of medical and began typing.

Penner glided over the floor as he walked. The male was smooth and graceful, and it reminded Rannn of a perfect predator. He stood behind Ansel and read the screen. At first, Penner just looked observationally curious. Then he narrowed his eyes and stepped closer.

"By all that is holy. What a beautiful virus. How did you create that?"

Ansel stopped, but he didn't look back. "I didn't."

Penner looked thoughtful. "Is that why I'm here. To help you recreate it or cure it?"

Ansel whipped around. "You're here to do the mundane tests that I don't have time for. These samples are private, and you do not have clearance to view the genetic coding."

Penner pursed his lips. "That was so long ago. I've moved passed that line of business."

"I don't care." Ansel turned back to his screen and began typing again. Rannn wondered if he would treat his brother the same way if he had one.

Probably.

Penner looked at Rannn with something in his expression that Rannn didn't recognize. "The sooner you figure out the Sennite problem, the quicker you can go back to your life."

"Never heard of Federation forcing non-Federation doctors to help. Is there a war I don't know about?"

Rannn felt the implication. It was a slight to his honor. Except he didn't think that he'd done anything dishonorable. Not even close. "Ansel's medical knowledge surpasses anyone else's in the Federation. He needed help, and you were the only one we could think of who might come close to his experience."

"Ansel and I do not specialize in the same...medical fields. He's more of a"—Penner rubbed his fingers together with one hand, searching for words—"biomechanical expert."

"And you're more of a fashion expert?" Clalls said from behind Rannn, still sitting on the medbed.

Penner turned around, but Rannn watched Ansel. Just as he thought, his friend was smirking again.

Seeing that eased some of Rannn's worries. Ansel would be okay. That smirk said volumes.

"I'm a microbiology expert, specializing in squirmy things that live in your blood." Penner grabbed a coat from the counter and pulled it on. "But in my spare time, I make emergency house calls. It pays the bills. And my tailor."

"For someone with a micro specialty, I would imagine you could get rid of your purple fingernails," Clalls said, sliding off the medbed.

"Sometimes, recognition goes a long way for intimate credibility."

"So do expensive-looking clothes." Clalls yawned as if the conversation were the most boring of his life. He gave Rannn a quick nod and then walked out.

"He reminds me of someone I know on Marnak. Except... Naff has black horns instead of big teeth. I wonder why rudeness is a Night Demon trait." Penner rubbed his chin as if he were trying to come up with a theory.

Rannn tapped the Minky pad that Penner should be paying attention to. "More working, less theorizing."

Penner gave him a look but didn't say anything.

Nue left her chair and walked to the other side of Penner. Rannn didn't like how far away she was. Even though they were having a silent fight, it didn't give her the right to keep her distance.

Nue's voice was poised and emotionless when she said, "I'm sure you don't need any help figuring out what's wrong. But I was born on Sennite, and I wondered if this world-wide sterilization thing might be from our birth control."

Penner turned to Rannn's wife and gave her a quick once-over before politely saying, "You're a hybrid Sennite." The male made a face, then said, "Terran. I can see some freckles. They're the only race with those things. As a hybrid, I can't imagine you'd know anything. The doctors wouldn't have given you any birth control because they wouldn't have kept you on the planet.

You would have been shipped off to be raised by someone else. Most likely, your Terran father."

Rannn was...stunned.

Nue was part Terran? Why did that make so much sense? And yet, it didn't. Rannn couldn't understand his feelings.

Nue avoided his eyes. Licking her lips, she added, "I'm aware of my non-Sennite half. But that does not mean I was shipped off as an infant. I was ten. I was on the planet long enough to see what the birth control did to my friends."

Penner tilted his head. "Ten years is a long time. Who is your mother?"

Nue shook her head. "That's irrelevant to the sterilization issue."

What? Who *was* her mother? Why was this female constantly keeping secrets from him?

Penner nodded. "So she's high-ranking. I assume your father was a lover she took without permission. Or was she given permission?"

"You're not listening to me," Nue said firmly. "We are talking about the planet-wide sterilization of the Sennites. I don't know if you're stalling on purpose because you know you can't figure it out, or are playing some Numan mind game. Either way, this conversation about my family is over. Fail fast and all that."

Nue didn't give him so much as a look as she exited the medical room.

Rannn had every intention of following her. But first, he moved to Penner, making sure to tower over him. His words were low and threatening as he said, "Disrespect my wife again, and you won't leave this ship alive."

Penner nodded. "Understood."

As Rannn turned to leave, Ansel stood in his way, a finger pointed at Rannn's arm. "When did that happen?"

Looking down, Rannn saw the black bones protruding from

his lower arm and knuckles. Raising it, he let Ansel take a good look. "Less than an hour after I left Clalls to watch you."

"Why didn't you tell me the bones broke through?" Ansel asked, clearly upset.

"I was...in the middle of something."

Ansel frowned, and then Rannn saw him comprehend.

"Interesting. But they weren't like that when you first walked in here."

"They retract when I'm not...worked up, I guess." Rannn assumed as much, anyway. At first, he'd figured it only happened when he was sexually stimulated. But after Penner had deliberately humiliated his wife, Rannn was ready to breathe fire, and out they popped.

Ansel peered at Sci, and they each got that look as if they were thinking about something. Then Ansel nodded. "Agreed."

Rannn waited.

"I'd like to wake up the rest of the crew and, as you say, work up their blood pressure. I figure a good sparring match should do it."

"You want them to progress? What if you could cure them before they finished turning into...this?"

Ansel looked away for a moment and whispered, "I'll be honest. I don't think I can fix this. I can't isolate where the mutations are inside the virus. But if the mutation can be...abated during times of calm, that might be worth spreading the word about."

Rannn was about to agree when Penner stepped up. "It causes a bone mutation. Okay, I'm going to need to be in on this."

Ansel scowled.

Rannn didn't know why Ansel was so against Penner's help. But Ansel had said it himself: he didn't understand why this was happening. Maybe Penner would.

With great control, Rannn calmed his heart rate and slowed his breathing. Concentrating on that focus, the black bones retracted.

Penner whistled.

Ansel frowned. "I'm going to wake up the rest of the Yunkin crew and see if they can all do what Rannn can."

"Sounds logical," Penner said as he rubbed his hands.

"I will send them down to the gym for their sparring session as soon as they wake up," Ansel said, still looking at Penner with skepticism.

"May I watch?" Penner asked.

Ansel didn't answer, but Rannn did. And he felt very Demon-esque as he told the male, "As soon as you figure out the Sennite problem."

Penner frowned, but he didn't look at the Minky pad. The Numan turned to follow Ansel. When he tried to cross behind the counter, the niskie advanced, exposing her teeth.

Penner snorted. "Ansel...get your pet."

Ansel pulled something out of the chiller and tossed it into the air. The niskie's yellow eyes glowed as its tongue shot out quickly. On the downward arch, the niskie caught a grey-looking...something in its mouth. "Good girl, Orna."

21

OUT OF CONTROL

In the ship's gym, Rannn smashed his fist into another officer's jaw, hearing the male bellow from the force of the hit compounded by the puncture wounds from Rannn's bone protrusions. The officer hit his knees before falling over.

Grey blood soaked his arms, and still, the fire inside him refused to settle. His lungs filled over and over as he looked for the next fighter.

No one.

All of them were on the floor, more broken than when they'd started, one with a broken horn, all bleeding, some unconscious. Finally. Now Rannn could go find his wife and talk to her about...what was it she was hiding from him again?

Oh, yeah, the fact that her mother was a high-ranking Sennite. He wanted to know who it was and why she hadn't told him. This time when they talked, he was going to do so in his office so he could listen to her entire past without distraction.

It was uncommon in a Yunkin union to know so little about a partner's bloodline. Not that this was that kind of marriage. But still, Nue was his, and she could have at least told him that she was a hybrid.

Hell, thinking about it now, he didn't even know how old she was. What if she was just a pup? Damn, he hoped not. He was already one hundred and twenty-one years old. He didn't want to be married a young twenty-year-old.

Scanning the Yunkins on the mat, Rannn saw they were mainly from Weapons and Tactical Response so they had been trained to fight. And they'd fought hard. But they all needed to go back to medical now.

He debated whether he should help them or tell Ansel to come and get them. He preferred to leave them so he could go find Nue.

From the far side of the gym, he heard clapping. Turning, he saw Clalls headed his way. When he stopped outside the fighting ring, Clalls used a finger to point to his arms. "Gotta say, Cap. I love the new look. Black bones are rare, even for Night Demons. Also, considered bad luck. But who cares about any of that?"

How long had Clalls been watching? "What do you want?"

"Me? Isn't this the Night Demon-Yunkin support meeting? Or is that next Thursday? I always forget."

It was very un-Yunkin to not take things seriously. That was probably why Clalls was so annoying to his past commanders and captains. There were pages and pages of complaints.

But for whatever reason, Clalls didn't bother Rannn now. Before he'd mutated, he respected Clalls—to a point—but he never felt at ease around him.

Maybe it wasn't that he felt easy. Perhaps it was that he didn't worry as much anymore.

Clalls stepped over the unconscious bodies, examining them closely. When he saw one officer with long teeth like he had, Clalls frowned. "I never thought I'd say this, but I look way better than he does with long teeth."

"It's just a temporary thing. He'll be back to himself soon."

The Demon didn't even look fazed as he continued stepping over bodies, eyeing them from head to toe.

"I heard that your bones retract."

The comment was so casual, Rannn almost missed it entirely. There was no way he could calm down enough to show Clalls, so he nodded instead.

The Night Demon made a sound and moved to the next body as if this were all normal.

"Ooo. I bet that hurt," he said, pointing at a broken horn. "The other Demons will respect him more, though." Clalls looked over with a smirk. "Demons respect battle scars."

"We're not Demons."

At that, Clalls stood up, and his expression turned sober, something Rannn had never seen before. "You of all people should be able to see the truth. You're already more Demon than you ever were. Even if Ansel removes the protrusions, you're still a Demon where it counts. I know you. You're predictably Yunkin. But the man I see now, he's a hybrid. And those idiots on the floor... I watched them and saw them take every cheap shot they could to take you down and extinguish their anger. They are not the same either."

"Trauma and stress can change any male. Yunkin or not. Being deformed will naturally cause the crew to fight out their problems. We are still just males."

Clalls' brows rose. "Maybe. But then again, what Yunkin captain would take a recently acquitted prisoner as his wife? Especially when he's expected to marry one of his own species and produce other pureblooded Yunkins to continue his long and respected bloodline."

"I make my own choices. I am my own male," Rannn said, refusing to give any further explanation.

"Exactly. You don't see yourself as part of a whole anymore.

That's a Yunkin concept. Demons are responsible to only themselves."

Rannn had not thought of it that way.

Clalls pulled a Minky pad out of his pocket and handed it to Rannn. "Yon called you three times. Couldn't get through, so he called me."

Rannn took the device and saw it was a call from Sands, not Yon. Rannn eyed the Demon, a little confused.

"And congratulations on your matehood," Clalls said, not answering Rannn's unspoken question.

It was the most insane comment Rannn had ever heard. And yet, it resonated as truth. He was mated.

"Who's mated?" Yon's voice carried through the Minky pad.

"I am," Rannn said as the door to the gym slid open from the far side of the room. Medscopes floated towards him. Ansel, Sci, and Penner must have decided the sparring match was done.

"Clalls, if you are pretending to be Rannn, I'm going to break your jaw when I get back."

Clalls rolled his eyes.

Rannn looked down at the black screen. "It's me, Yon. And I took Nue as my wife."

There was silence for a beat, and then a quiet, "Okay. I... congratulations, then," Yon stuttered awkwardly.

"I'm sure you called for a reason," Rannn said as he grabbed the first medscope and handed it to the Yunkin with half his jaw scraped off.

"I did, yes," Yon said with a stronger voice. One that sounded more comfortable. "First things first. Everyone is alive."

Rannn stood back up and grabbed another floating medscope to hand out. "Does that mean the mission has been completed?"

"Depends on your definition of complete. If you hoped to

have Calum in chains and ready for interrogation, then no, that mission failed. But we did find his ship."

Rannn pursed his lips as he continued handing out the medscopes, noticing that Clalls wasn't helping at all. In fact, he was pulling another Minky pad out of his pocket and typing on the screen furiously.

"Why don't you start at the beginning and tell me what happened?"

"Why do you sound so calm about our failure?"

Rannn looked at his arm that was now absent its series of black protruding bones. "Long day. But before you start your debrief, tell me, have you been feeling any bone-deep pains?"

"Uh. No. Why would I?"

So it was a Yunkin-only disease. Neither Clalls nor Yon had had reactions. "No reason. Okay, go ahead with the report."

Clalls snickered, and Rannn could only imagine that the Demon was displeased with Rannn for double-checking to see if Yon might have the mutation.

"Okay, well, the first part was routine. The flight went pretty fast, and it was easy to find the ship. Chollar left Jandy on our ship so he could be bait. Like we planned. But the same drills that attacked us in the Outworlds attacked his ship. Chollar took on the drills and Calum's ship at the same time. Both vessels were destroyed. Chollar escaped via evo-suit. He used his abilities to fly back to our ship. As he came our way, Vivra ran infrared on the ship and debris and found a single person in a lifepod. No one else was alive."

Rannn looked around at the slowly healing bodies and decided it was time to leave. As he did, Clalls was right beside him.

Rannn gave him a look, but the male just shrugged. "And Chollar didn't know there was a living person in a lifepod?"

"He said that the person inside was in a deep state of unconsciousness. In other words, Chollar didn't hear the person's thoughts. Vivra thinks it's Calum. But looking over the scans, the person inside looks young."

Rannn rubbed his face as he entered the elevator. "It might be Calum. Don't open it, there could be diseases inside."

"I thought of that, too. And even if it's not Calum, and he got away, he could be diseased. We tried to grab some of the ship's memory core to bring to Sands and Lita."

That all sounded good.

"But everything was blackened as if it had been burned from the inside—long before we got there."

Rannn entered his office and half-expected Nue inside. When he found it empty, he checked the cabin just in case.

Empty.

She was somewhere on the ship. He didn't like not knowing where she was. The fact that she wasn't *home* made him crave her more.

Rannn touched his Minky screen and moved the call from the Minky pad to the larger monitor. He pushed his personal issues out of his mind and focused on the black screen.

Clalls took a seat and leaned back, making himself comfortable.

"When shall I expect you back?"

"That's why I'm calling. We need a ship. Chollar found a drifting spaceport. Its environment is up and running. But it's junk. I'm sure if Sands was here, he could make a ship out of all the scraps on this heap, but we can't. So, we need a ride out."

Rannn didn't bother sending a message. In his mind, he called Sci's name. An image of the Cerebral popped in his head. *Yon and the crew need a pickup. I'll send you the coordinates soon.*

The image nodded and disappeared.

"What's the manufacturing model of the spaceport?" Clalls asked, leaning forward.

"No idea," Yon replied. "But two guys were stranded on the port after their ship broke down. They have been trying to fix it up. But I'll be honest, if this is what two years of work looks like....it's never getting its space legs."

Clalls tapped his fingers on the desk as if he were thinking about that. Rannn didn't know why, but it didn't bother him. "Send me and Sasha the coordinates, they are on their way."

"That's the thing, I have no idea where we are. This is a drifting pile of scrap, and the idiots who are fixing it up don't have a working communication system."

"If you are on a pile a scrap, how are you transmitting this call?"

"In short? Sands is transmitting my message to him through the ship's call log. I can connect to Sands whenever I want—a feature Ansel added to our cybernetic pathways."

"Can Sands use that link to find you?"

"I don't think so. I have no idea where Sands is right now."

Clalls cleared his throat loudly and tossed his other Minky pad towards Rannn. "I chipped Vivra after she returned from Brica when she almost died. There are the coordinates."

Rannn looked at the pad and then at Clalls, impressed as hell. "You absolutely deserve that raise."

Clalls leaned back like he owned the room. "Commander Clalls does have a sweet ring to it."

Rannn read off the numbers in his mind to ensure that Sci got them correct. The telepath had a photographic memory and wouldn't forget. As soon as Rannn relayed the directions to Sci he also told him to bring Sands and Lita just in case.

Sci popped into his head again and nodded in agreement.

"Done." Rannn told Yon, "I've let Sasha know to bring the mechanics."

"Great. Then I will see you in a few days. I hope."

Rannn nodded and, instead of telling Yon to stay safe like he wanted, he terminated the call. The mission was a bust. No Calum. No easy access to a cure.

Clalls stood up from his seat with an odd expression of amusement.

"You seem pleased with yourself. But, understandable. You did well." Rannn pulled up the document needed to promote an officer.

"I chipped Vivra because she was my friend. That wasn't even trying. But...that spaceport sure did sound interesting. A male like me could do a lot of things with an abandoned space-port. I might have to check it out when this is all over."

Rannn never saw this side of Clalls. "Yon said people are fixing it up, so it's not exactly abandoned."

"He said two people. Idiots, actually. I doubt they have my kind of vision." Clalls sounded almost wistful.

Rannn sat down, seeing the real Clalls for maybe the first time. The calculating Demon, who saw what he wanted and then meticulously planned to conquer it.

"Well, my work here is done." Pointing at the document, Clalls added, "I look forward to the well-deserved promotion. Please don't forget to add in a little note about how I went well above and beyond the call of duty."

"I know how to fill them out, thank you."

Clalls made a face before exiting. Rannn completed the rest of the questions and added the justification part regarding how well Clalls responded when time was of the essence.

The quantum network was down, so it wouldn't go through to Admiral Orin, but Rannn saved it and set it aside to send as soon as the system was back up.

Then he remembered that he needed to fill out a marriage document and update his status. That took longer than he planned. Also, the update would wait in his queue until the network returned. But at least his ship-wide status was now updated.

An image of Sci popped into his head. Then a picture of Nue. She was near the lifepods, trying to gain access. The image disappeared just as quickly as it came. Rannn was out of the office less than a heartbeat later.

His lungs burned as he pushed his speed as fast as he could. Fear fueled him.

22

MATED

Nue hated this ship. Nothing worked. What if they were being attacked? She would need to evacuate somehow. Why did she need to enter in a Federation ID to escape?

Stupid.

"Nue."

No. Seth of Stars, she didn't want to hear whatever crap he was about to say. He'd made it damn clear that he wasn't happy about her comments to Penner. He didn't even stand up for her questions. Not that she needed him to. But his silence hurt.

Then worse, he never came to check on her.

Which was why she was here, trying to get off this stupid ship. Because if he was affected by something as ridiculous as her speaking her thoughts and being half Terran, then he would never accept the fact that she was a felon.

"What are you doing by the lifepods?"

"You're a smart guy. You know."

"Come here." Rannn held out his hand.

Nue stuffed her hands into her pockets. "No. What do you want?"

"I want you to come here and tell me why you think it's okay to leave. Less than a day into our marriage, and you want to call it quits. I don't think so."

Nue backed up and turned towards the opening to the cargo bay. She needed more space, and she needed air. "It's funny you think I am calling it quits, considering the first thing *you* said after waking up with me was to warn me not to use your rank as mine. A truly scathing thing to say to a wife of only a few hours. But wait,"—she held up a finger—"we're not officially married. I had it checked. Your status doesn't say we're married."

Rannn was silent for a moment and dropped his hand, his emotions schooled. She hated it.

His voice was soft. "You're my wife, Nue."

"Apparently, not. Because if I were, then you would put in the paperwork. You would have come to see if your wife was okay. But you didn't because you don't care."

He moved closer, and she stepped back. His voice even softer, he said, "You're my wife, and I apologize for making you feel unwanted. And I did update my status just now. You can check. The document is filled out and in my message queue. And as soon as the Yunkin quantum network is back up, it will go straight to Admiral Orin to acknowledge it."

Rannn held out his hand, and she moved away from it.

"Don't bother sending anything, I won't sign it."

"You already said yes. Spoken words to a captain are binding."

"You're not my captain," she hissed, hitting the elevator button. She needed to get away from him before she did something stupid like tell him how much she wanted to be his wife.

"Nue, I'm sorry I didn't come sooner."

The elevator opened, and she rushed forward.

Hard arms wrapped around her stomach, and she

screamed, fearing that his black-boned mutations would cut into her skin. His head by hers, he held her off the floor, hushing her.

Nue kicked and jerked her head back, hoping to free herself.

"Nue, I had to help the other Yunkins. I had to help them progress with their mutations so it stopped hurting them. I am still a captain, and I didn't stay away from you to hurt you. I did it to help my crew."

"Crew before Nue...what a marriage."

Rannn growled as he pressed her up against the inside of the elevator cab. His mouth by her ear, he said, "With Seth as my witness, I did not put you second. I am a captain, *and* I am your husband. I am both. And I will not let you shame me for doing my job. You knew who I was and what I was when you agreed to this union. I will give you all of myself and my time when I can, but I am also a captain and responsible for thousands of lives. Should I have just resigned? Would that have made it better for you?"

His words cut deep. Remorse pricked her soul for making him doubt his position. But she was just so hurt.

"Nue."

"I waited for you," she whispered, feeling the knot in her throat start to sting.

His body hugged her tighter. His voice sweeter. "Nue, I'm sorry. I'm sorry you thought I didn't want you. I could never leave you. Never. Both my Yunkin and Demon side have claimed you."

Both his what and...what?

"What does that mean?"

Rannn kissed the crux of her neck and shoulder from the back. He nipped the skin before sucking it into his mouth. "It means you're my everything. Wife. Mate. The future mother of our children."

Her knees dipped. He was serious. She had to tell him. "Rannn, I can't be your wife."

"You already are."

"But there's something you don't know, and you need to."

"That your mother is a high-ranking Sennite? I don't care, you're still mine."

"No. My mother's not high-ranking. But my aunt is Admiral Livanna. But I never knew her and my mom turned me over to my father when she decided I was too soft hearted. She means nothing. What you need to know is...I am actually a felon."

When Rannn's heat receded, she wanted to cry. He turned her around, face looking every bit like a captain and not her husband. She wished she'd stayed silent, but she couldn't keep this from him."

"Are you telling me that you killed that male?"

"No." Seth of Stars, how could he think that? How could he even question that? Didn't he know her? No. He couldn't have. Honestly, they didn't know anything about each other.

Knowing this was the end, she cast her eyes to the side and brought up the memory and told him, "I caught an article about a cargo ship crashing into a moon at light speed. The ship was on a Federation path, and no one understood how a moon could just float into the trajectory. When I looked it up and inspected that part of space, I noticed that the flight paths were old, and some were downright dangerous. So I...fixed them."

Rannn's voice was quiet but still very captain-like. "You broke into the system. That's how they caught you and punished you."

She didn't dare look at him. She could feel her throat burn with too much emotion. "So, I can't be with you because I am a felon and I deserve..." She couldn't say the word *Debsa* because she violently didn't want to die there.

Tears crested her lids, and her chest shook.

Rannn reached down and grabbed her hand as the elevator pinged. She didn't even know they were traveling. How did she miss that?

Reading the level, she realized they were back at Rannn's office and cabin. He pulled her out, and all she could think about was how badly she'd just messed up. He sat her down on the Minky table and pulled her legs apart so he could get closer. He held her face in his hands and brushed a thumb over her cheek.

His voice soft—his *husband* voice—he said, "I didn't think I could be more proud of you for your abilities. But knowing that you broke into the Federation maps to fix what was broken shows me how much honor you have. As your husband, you can be sure that I will find out the name of the tarq who judged you unfairly. And I will make it right."

She tried to shake her head. There was no way to make it right. Rannn couldn't change what an admiral had decided.

She looked at his arm. The spikes were out and longer than before. "Nue. Trust me to take care of you. Trust me to never leave you or this marriage."

He was crazy. They weren't even married.

Rannn pulled her forehead to his lips. Then he kissed her cheeks before he tilted her head back so her mouth was open for him. His blue eyes were dark and serious. "You are going to learn that relationships are not perfect. I will make mistakes, and so will you. But at no time are we going to give up. It's you and me forever."

"Promise?"

Rannn's voice was harsh and guttural with emotion. "I promise."

"Thank you," was all she could say.

Her husband's jaw tightened, and she saw him fighting something. But he didn't voice what it was. Instead, he grabbed her neck and pulled her mouth to his. He pushed in his tongue and devoured and claimed.

He chanted her name as he removed her clothes. He told her exactly what he wanted to do to her body and how much he needed her. Then he grabbed her and threw her over his shoulder.

Inside the cabin, Rannn put her on the bed and instructed, "On your stomach, now."

She crawled up onto the bed and lay arms-up, just the way he liked. Her lady parts were wet and needy. She felt his fingers at her entrance first. He pushed inside, and she ground against his hand.

"My wife knows me, and she trusts me. Doesn't she?"

His damn games.

"Please."

He pushed in again. This time, he added pressure to the bundle of nerves between her folds. "My wife knows me and trusts me to take care of her body and her heart. Doesn't she?"

When she didn't say anything, Rannn withdrew his hand. She could feel him climb onto the bed and lean over her. His mouth by her ear, he slowly let some of his weight rest on top of her.

"You're going to learn to trust me with everything," he said just as she felt the silky tip push inside.

He filled her and pumped until she was almost there, almost at her climax. She reached for it. When he lowered himself down on top of her and continued to rut, she found she couldn't breathe.

He didn't stop.

"Rannn?"

He didn't stop, he just thrust harder and stronger, and she was...she was... Oh, damn. She was going to come. Grabbing the blanket, she dug in her nails. Her chest burned, but so did her womb.

Almost.

Almost.

"RANNN," she grunted as she was plunged into a world of darkness and bliss. Her entire being was filled with white-hot pleasure that she couldn't understand. She couldn't grasp anything but that it felt amazing. Then Rannn lifted up enough to give her air before he moved back down and continued to plunder.

He dominated her body until she came again. But instead of giving her air, he stayed until she whimpered.

"My wife trusts me," he said between thrusts. "Trust me, damn it."

That's when she got it.

She had been trying to push up to keep breathing, and he was asking her to stop trying. To trust him to know her body.

Lowering her head, she let her self go limp.

Rannn's forehead touched the back of her neck. His weight was lighter; she could breathe. "My wife trusts me."

"She trusts you," Nue said, amazed that marriage to Rannn was like this.

He kissed the back of her neck as he pulled out and flipped her over, then he moved to face her as he guided himself back inside. Her thighs came up naturally, and she was pleased that she could now see his face.

Brushing her thumb over his lips, she felt him thrust inside.

"Your wife loves how you feel inside."

Rannn covered her mouth for a kiss then started to really give it to her. She didn't know how he had the stamina, but damn if he didn't give her two more climaxes. There might have been a third, but she was exhausted by the end.

Her husband was obviously living up to her dreams.

Her mind a warm fog of tingles, she fell asleep face-down on his chest, praying to Seth that nothing would happen to her new husband.

Because she was falling in love with him, and she wanted him forever.

And no one had ever made her feel so whole or so wanted before.

23

MAYDAY MAYDAY

Rannn carefully moved Nue to the pillow and slid out from under her. His wife was completely out. Which was exactly what he planned, but he kind of thought it would take longer. He wondered if she knew how easy it was to make her come.

Not that he minded. But he pondered whether she also felt the raw emotions from before, when she'd thought that he didn't want her. When she confessed her biggest secret without being asked. It was so absurd, it floored him.

Marriage was not something he'd offered because he wanted her body. He did it because she was the one. She felt right. She felt like his.

He didn't realize just how much she worried and cared until he saw her tears. As foolish as it was, he'd thought he was the one who'd felt the pull. But the look of devastation on her face at being rejected was astounding. Wounding.

Rannn kissed her head before grabbing his clothes, dressing quickly to exit the cabin.

He powered up the Minky table in his office, and in very clear writing, wrote her a note she would see the second she walked out of the cabin. Rannn had thought he'd made himself clear that he cared about her. That he wanted her. But this note would add to the foundation.

He took the trip to the medical bay, expecting an update. He didn't expect to find a room full of pissed off Yunkins, who were yelling at Ansel from across the room—Orna, the niskie, the barrier between them.

Rannn inhaled and whistled as loudly as he could.

The guards turned their gazes on him. He glared back. "What in the name of Seth do you think you're doing, yelling at your commander?"

"He's supposed to fix us. He's not fixing us," one with horns on his forehead said.

"You think he can fix anything with you yelling at him?" Rannn shot back.

"How long are we supposed to wait? Why can't he just shave it off? It can't be that hard," said another Yunkin with long tusks protruding from the sides of his jaw.

"Shaving it won't change the Demon part of you," said Clalls, who sat with an ankle over his knee, looking unfazed. Rannn had no idea why Clalls was in the medical bay, but at this point, he'd give the new commander a modicum of trust.

"Shut up, Clalls. I'm not a Demon," snapped the Yunkin with the tusks.

"Says the male who is rioting in the medical bay with protruding mandible bones. Short ones...I might add. Trust me, it's not a good look. Those Demons with jawbone mutations always reminded me of a lizard."

A lizard. He liked that. He might have to call the guy *Lizzard*. Rannn snorted at Clalls, understanding the Demon's motivations more and more.

"Ignore the idiot," said Lizzard. "Captain, just tell Ansel to remove the bones, and we'll leave."

Rannn scratched his jaw. "Oh, is that all?"

A female Yunkin pointed at Rannn. "Why isn't he...why doesn't he have protruding bones like us? Is he cured? That's not fair. Ansel cured him and not us."

Rannn didn't know all their names, but it was clear that he had to take action. "You know what I find interesting? Why none of you are at your appointed jobs. Or is today a Seth holiday? Maybe I got my days mixed up."

"I think you're thinking of Rubar's Day, Cap. That's next month," Clalls said from the side of the room, clearly enjoying this.

None of the other Yunkins laughed. Pity. If they had, they would have understood what Rannn was trying to get them to figure out for themselves.

"Captain. Clearly, you of all people can understand why we need this. You've obviously already been cured or had your bone mutations removed. We can't stay like this," Horns said.

Rannn shrugged. "You're alive. Be thankful."

"This is not living, I look like a freak," said Lizzard. "I'll be disowned."

Rannn tapped his temple. "Clue in. *All* Yunkins are like this. All purebloods. How could you be disowned when your family will have the same or similar mutations?"

"That can't be true. I don't believe you," said Horns.

"I should have a choice to remove these damn things. I refuse to look like any of *them*," Lizzard said.

Rannn held out his arms. "When did our race become so vain? So racist. Are we not taught to honor each other and everyone else? Are we not taught to value everyone and treat individuals the same?"

Horns stepped forward. "No, I was not taught that. We are better. We are Yunkin. The Demons are a race cursed by Seth of Stars."

Rannn felt his heart mourn. That was not what it was to be a Yunkin. "You were taught wrong. We are all flesh and blood."

"They are deceivers. Game players. No one trusts the Demons."

Scanning the faces, Rannn asked, "Do you all feel this way?"

One Yunkin that had previously been quiet in the back, dropped his eyes before stepping out. "My mother taught me to value everyone equally. But in the academy, I started to think like the rest of my friends." Rannn saw that the male's nails had turned into claws.

Rannn held up a finger and called him forward. "What's your name?"

"Oz."

"Come with me," Rannn said and walked out of the medical bay, wondering if he could get the male to calm down enough for the mutations to retract. It was just a guess, but he wanted to try. He made sure to speak his intentions so Sci could hear and convey to Ansel.

A moment later, he saw a picture of Sci in his mind, next to Ansel. Both were holding a thumb up.

Out in the hall, Rannn had the young male wait as he held up his arm. Then he punched the wall as hard as he could. Pain and anger unleashed inside of him, and the black bones emerged.

Oz jumped back. "Holy Seth. How did you do that?"

Rannn didn't answer. Instead, he jerked his chin and said, "Walk with me and tell me about how you came to my crew. And then I'll tell you how."

Oz reached back to rub his neck but scratched himself instead. "Um. Okay." Oz frowned at his hands before letting them fall. "I don't know what you want to know exactly."

"Start with your family. Are both parents Federation?"

"No," he said as if embarrassed by that fact.

"Your mother stayed home with you and brought you up herself?" Rannn guessed.

Oz nodded.

"That was selfless of her. My mother did the same while my sister and I were in our infancy. She didn't go back to work as a professor until we were older."

Oz almost smiled. "My mom likes to bake. She makes these blue flower cookies. Sometimes, she sends me a few batches."

Rannn could tell that, somewhere in there, Oz felt bad about something. But he didn't comment. Instead, he just let the boy talk. And talk. And talk.

They walked the distance from one end of the level to the other and then took the elevator to the next and did it again. It was a long while before the topic transitioned into Oz's time at school. That's when Rannn learned that there had been groups of students enforcing their beliefs. Oz had had a hard time fitting in until he just went along with it.

After that, the boy broke down.

During his open confessions, Rannn noticed that the Yunkin's claws had receded. His gut instinct had been right.

Rannn watched as the elevator door opened, and Nue walked out. In her hand, she held two pouches of something. Oz wiped his eyes and went quiet as she approached.

"Here, I thought you might be thirsty. I saw you walking for a while."

"Thank you," Rannn said to his wife. Her thoughtfulness would not be forgotten. Also, the sleepy look in her eyes made him want to kiss her. But right now, he was acting as the captain, not a husband.

Oz took the pouch. "Thank you, ma'am."

Rannn's wife smiled. "Love his manners."

Rannn nodded at her, and she took that as her cue to leave.

Once she was out of earshot, Oz said, "I don't know her. Is she new to the crew?"

"She's been released from duty."

"Oh." Oz looked almost sad. "She's nice. It's too bad we're losing her."

"Well, she's my wife, so she's not leaving."

Oz's eyes widened. "I didn't know you were married."

"It's fairly recent."

"Oh," Oz said again, looking down for a moment. Suddenly, it was like something came over him, and his back straightened. "I think you have a great wife. And I'm glad you are keeping her with you. I know my mom always wished my father had brought her along. She always told me how much she missed him."

"I'm glad you agree," Rannn said, holding up his water and taking a drink. He finished the contents in one gulp. When he lowered the bag, he noticed Oz hadn't drunk any of his. The boy was looking at his hand, or rather, his lack of claws.

Oz's eyes were hazy when they turned to Rannn. "How did you do it?"

"Not me, Oz. You. You have to be at peace to make the abnormalities recede. But if you have hate, anger, obsessive thoughts, or are feeling any very heightened emotion, they come back."

Oz looked back down to his hand. "I *am* at peace." The words were said in awe, almost like he didn't know what that meant.

"Do you think the others will change, too?"

Honestly, Rannn didn't think all of them could. But he was going to try. "It's up to them. Ready to go show them your new trick?"

Oz looked at his hand, and the claws came back.

A minute later, they left.

"Hell yeah, I'm ready."

Boys.

As PREDICTED, not all the crewmembers were able to make their abnormalities recede at will. In fact, only two others could, and that left the rest pretty damn pissed. But Rannn didn't sugarcoat it when he told them, "This curse, this mutation, can be healed. The only person keeping it from happening is you. Think on that."

In addition to that, he told the crew that unless they weren't able to work anymore, they'd better get back to their jobs. This was not a cruise ship.

To Clalls, he said, "Get a hold of Sol and bring back the rest of the crew. The ship is clean, and there is no more biohazard. Also, check on Sasha. See where she is and find out how long until the remaining crew gets back. Then, meet me on the bridge."

"On it," he said, leaving the medical bay with a light bounce to his step.

Before Rannn left, he made sure that everyone was gone. To Penner, he asked, "I assume you found out what caused the problem on the planet?"

"I did. Mostly."

Rannn propped his hands on his hips, waiting.

"Your wife was right. It was the birth control."

"Can you fix it?"

Penner winced. "Uh. No. I would have to implant synthetic wombs in every female over the age of twelve."

Rannn dropped his hands. "Two uncurable issues that affected an entire planet. What are the odds?"

Penner looked at Ansel. "Unlikely. All of it was most likely caused on purpose."

"I agree," Ansel said without the usual heat to his voice.

"And neither of them is curable?"

Penner looked away. Ansel shook his head.

"Well, we're still alive. And that's all that matters." Or at least that was all that mattered to Rannn. He already had scars from being used as an arena fighter. His skin was already blemished. What was a little more?

But the guards with unmarred skin and respected bloodlines were not taking the change well. And the Sennites were going to reject their diagnosis. Rannn was not looking forward to speaking with the planet's admiral.

RANNN SAT in his captain's chair in the bridge, waiting for Clalls to get the planet admiral on the Minky. She had rejected all his calls for the past hour.

In addition, Rannn tried to speculate on who would be able to do this to his people—if not Calum.

Looking at the Minky screen, he observed the clock that Clalls had put up to let him know precisely when Yon and the crew would be back. They were still eight hours out.

Rannn tapped the side of his chair, wondering why he was so...stirred up. It was as if he knew something was wrong but couldn't figure out what.

He went over all the people and topics he could think of.

Clalls grunted as he slapped his console. "She's not answering on purpose. I can literally see her staring at her screen. Look," he said, pointing at the image. Rannn didn't bother to ask if Clalls had hacked into the planet admiral's Minky, because it was obvious. "I vote you just send her a message saying: *Sorry you're sterile, it's all your fault. Respectfully, Captain Rannn.*"

"Do you have a way to force a message?"

"Not legally."

"Do it anyway."

Clalls hit several buttons and then turned around and pointed at Rannn.

"Admiral Livanna, this is Captain Rannn. I have been informed that the cause of the sterilization is your birth control. My doctors will be sending you the report in the next hour."

Rannn could see the admiral staring at her screen with unmasked and horrified rage.

"There is no cure, but my doctors assured me that synthetic wombs could be used if so desired."

"How dare you hack my system, you uncivilized male? This is my private time, and I will not be called on like some... crewmember. I *am a planet admiral*. You will show me respect."

"Your planet needs your attention, and you want *private time*? You gave that up when you accepted the responsibility of all of the lives under your care."

Livanna hissed. "Don't you dare lecture me on how to run my planet, you simpleton."

"I'm not lecturing you. If you feel offended, that's your problem. Mine was to solve the mystery of the sterilization. I did that. Now, I'm done. The rest is on you."

Livanna roared. "Get off my Minky this instant, or I will have your rank by tomorrow."

She obviously hadn't noticed that the quantum network was down. Showed how much she was paying attention.

Rannn nodded at Clalls, and the Demon shut down the call.

"Glad that's over with," Clalls said.

Sol, who was sitting at his station, held up both hands as if he'd accidentally touched something he shouldn't have.

"Oh, damn. Oh, no."

"Sol?" Rannn called.

"Uh..." Sol peered over to Clalls. "Did we call for a mayday?"

"As if," Clalls shot back.

Sol pointed at his screen. "There is a huge armada headed our way."

Clalls stood up at the same time that Rannn did. Walking to the screen, they both peered over Sol's shoulder, one on each side. The infrared monitor confirmed that thousands of sloops were indeed headed their way. *And hundreds of battleships.*

Clalls walked back to his station, punched in a number, then waited. "This is Communications Officer Clalls. Want to tell me why the hell you're stalking my ship on silent mode?"

No response.

Clalls held up a finger to his lips then punched another number into the communication screen. "Hello, scrumptious. Want to tell me what you're doing heading towards the Garna?"

"How the hell did you get through without me even hearing my Minky pad ring?" a hushed female voice asked.

Clalls huffed. "Aw, scrumptious, I'm not calling to catch up. I got you that information you wanted last year. Now, you will return the favor. Why are you headed towards my ship?"

The Minky's speaker picked up a door shutting and then another one opening and closing. The voice echoed as if the female were in a small space. "If anyone finds out I told you, I'm not going to Debsa for you."

"Scrumptious…" Clalls warned, and Rannn liked seeing this serious yet still playful side to Clalls.

"Okay. So, a week or so ago, all the Yunkins came down with some crazy illness that made them all look like Night Demons. But worse, they were like wild beasts, getting pissed off over everything. So, Marggy had them all sent to their rooms under medical quarantine."

Clalls opened his mouth as if he were about to say something when the female added, "But this morning, Marggy got a message from an admiral ordering all Yunkins to be locked in their rooms or the brig. Then he was ordered to join up with an armada so they could rescue the other ships—you know, with Yunkin captains."

Clalls raised his brows. "When you say rescue, scrumptious, is that your word? Or was that in the message?"

"Mine. I think it officially said something like: *Remove from duty.*"

"Anything else I should know?"

"No."

Clalls rolled his eyes and terminated the call. "Well, there's your answer. The armada is plucking up Yunkin crews, starting with yours, I assume."

Rannn rubbed his mouth. "I wonder which admiral sent that message."

Clalls held up another finger as he sat down and began typing. About five minutes later, he stopped and pointed at the screen. "The biggest ship in the armada is the Killamire. According to this updated manifest, Admiral Armsono is on it."

Clalls and Sol turned to him, eyes leery because they understood exactly what that meant. Armsono was coming to take over.

Standing straight, Rannn said, "Bastard."

Sol sat down, his green scales lightening with worry. "If Armsono takes over the Garna, everything will get really bad."

Clalls snickered. "Sol, stop sniveling. You're a Bolark, for Seth's sake. Act like one for a change. And Armsono can't take over because he's a council admiral."

Sol hissed. "I'm serious. You don't know him like I do."

"And you do?" Clalls challenged.

"Yeah, I do. I know what he does with people when he knows they can't retaliate. When they know that no one will believe them."

Clalls went silent for a moment then said, "Why are you still letting the past get in your head? That time is over, you're here, and the scariest bastard you know is looking right at you."

"You're not scary, Clalls," Sol said.

"You have no idea because I don't play with little fish. You're not worth my time," Clalls snarked. To Rannn, the Demon said, "But seriously, Sol is right. If Armsono is leading the charge, we're screwed. He's a cheating bastard. He will shoot first and sort the bodies later. I know I'm not his favorite, but you're definitely on Armsono's I-want-to-destroy list."

Rannn didn't doubt for a minute that Clalls had had contact with Armsono. The Demon had taken the decimation of the Eldon planet pretty badly. Furthermore, Clalls had probably never been more honest than when he'd told Sol that he didn't deal with little fish.

But it was that comment that made Rannn think about Armsono's motivations. Addressing both males, he said, "What are the odds that Armsono is heading our way first to take me on because he thinks I'm the biggest...fish?"

Clalls hummed to himself. "Not the biggest fish. Wrong analogy. But if you think scathy barbist... Cut off the head, and the body shrivels up. Then, yes, I agree."

"Garna has the biggest and most advanced weapons. If he takes you down, he can use the Garna to scare the other captains into stepping down," Sols agreed.

Clalls rolled his eyes. "That's not it, infant. It's the crew that makes a ship. We have the most select crew in the Federation. Think about it. There's me—obviously—and then two Cerebrals, a Numan, two Numan-crafted cyborgs. Seriously, it's like the dream team."

"I think you should have stopped at the two Cerebrals," Sol said sarcastically.

Clalls' skin greyed as he scowled.

Rannn said, "Sol, don't underestimate Clalls. He's a Night

Demon who knows most if not all the admirals' deep dark secrets, *and* he keeps a Rana on retainer."

The Bolark's jaw dropped.

Clalls dismissed the Bolark with a wave of his hand. "She's not on retainer. She and I used to date. It didn't work out. So now I pay her to do things I know she wants to do."

It was Rannn's turn to be taken aback. Part of Rannn didn't want to believe it because...who would date a contract killer? But then, it sounded exactly like something Clalls would do.

Rannn walked back to his seat and checked the time clock for when Yon would be back. "How much time do we have until Armsono's armada gets here?"

Sol checked. "Six hours."

"Clalls, how many other ships have Yunkin captains?"

Clalls started typing on his Minky screen. "Forty-six."

"Are all their quantum networks still down?"

"What are you thinking? To send a mayday?" Clalls asked.

Rannn snorted. "No. But we can get Armsono on a call. We can broadcast it to the other ships. Let them know what's going on and prepare them in case we fail."

"We invite them to the party... I like that idea. The more, the merrier and all that," Clalls said.

A look of hope flooded the Bolark's eyes. "I like that idea, too."

24

DEAD OR ALIVE

Nue was in the captain's cabin, sitting on the bed with a Minky pad that her husband had given her. He'd said it was one of the ship's unused ones. He'd programmed it with his sister's ID. A sibling Nue didn't even know he had until an hour ago.

Nue understood that there was likely more about Rannn than she didn't know yet, but it felt weird when it was a person. Then again, Rannn had never met her father or sister. Not that he would ever meet Nova.

That kind of depressed Nue. She wished that she had a true Terran family with sisters and brothers and grandparents. Big families always seemed happier.

Just then, the Minky pad pinged with a call.

Nue sat back, worried about taking a call from a person looking for Rannn's sister. She let it ring five times before restarting her documentary about decorating cabins. A moment later, the Minky pinged again.

Nue hoped that Rannn's sister would get it, but she didn't.

On the third call, Nue's stomach twisted. Wincing, she

turned away from the screen. "Stop calling," she whispered to the unnamed caller.

When it finished, her stomach didn't settle.

Another ping, but this one was a message. A box dropped down on her screen for a moment to show a preview.

It read: *NoobyNue where r you*?

Nue stopped breathing. "Nova?"

The Minky pad chimed again with another call, and Nue quickly accepted it. The screen faded from the home improvement show to an almost mirror image of herself. Except, instead of Nue's black hair, the caller's was colored red and long.

And instead of Nue's magnetic blue-grey eyes that she achieved with contacts, Nova's natural purple orbs stared back at her.

"Hi, baby sister."

Really? "Fifteen minutes later does not make me the baby."

"It really does."

"No, it really doesn't."

"I'm older, so you have to listen to me," Nova said. Before Nue could answer, Nova leaned into the screen. "You need to leave that ship. Now."

Nue didn't want to admit that she couldn't. First, she didn't have a Federation ID to work the lifepods. And second, she was married to the captain.

"I saw that your fake ID was terminated. I have another one. Memorize this number—"

Nue cut her off. "I'm not leaving."

"Yes, you are. There is an *armada* headed straight for that ship. They plan to hit the Garna first because Rannn has the best defenses. They plan to arrest all the Yunkins. If anyone fights back, they *will* kill them."

"What?"

Nova nodded as she bit her lip. "I saw several Bolarks

executing scores of Yunkins at the docks. And all they were doing was fighting to leave the planet. The Bolarks think all the Yunkins are diseased and losing their minds. And I hate to take their side, but whatever happened to that race messed with their heads, too."

Nue felt a wave of possessiveness as she defended her husband. "They were turned into Night Demon hybrids. Yunkins are feeling Demon emotions. But it is not making them crazy."

Nova waved a hand as if she were done with the conversation. "It really doesn't matter. Right now, you matter, and you need to get off that ship. Now, memorize this number."

"No. I'm not leaving. I have a husband, and I will not leave him."

Nova's face fell. "What the hell did you just say to me? You're married? To whom!"

Nue sat up straight. "Rannn."

Nova's nostrils flared. "The bloody captain? Are you serious, Nue? You can't be married to *him*. He's diseased. And even if he wasn't, he's an arrogant, prick-faced Yunkin."

"He's my *husband,*" Nue hissed. "And I'm not leaving him. If ships are headed this way, he will protect us all. Because that's what he does." Nue thought back to the last mission she'd gone on. Of course, her memories consisted mostly of being stuck in his room, but that was because Rannn had been trying to keep her safe.

During the last mission, they'd lost a deadly shadow on the ship, then were attacked by space pirates, then went up against a cybernetic evil genius and won. If she had learned nothing else, she knew that staying with Rannn was the safest bet.

But to be fair, that wasn't why she wanted to stay. It was because she wanted to be Rannn's wife. She wanted to be by his side until the end. She wanted to love him as deeply as Hettens loved their mates.

"I get that you think so, but nobody can stop an entire armada. Do you understand how many ships that is?" Nova said as she pulled on her hair. "I didn't save you all those times for you to just sit there and die now with a husband you've known for a few weeks."

"Months," Nue corrected. But only to be argumentative, because, in essence, it had only been weeks.

"Look at my face," Nova said, pointing at herself. "Does it look like I'm kidding? Does it look like I'm giving you an option? DOES IT?"

Nue winced at the fervor in her sister's tone.

"Now, do as I say and memorize this number, and then use it on the lifepod and get off that ship. The lifepod will take you to Marnak, and I will have someone pick you up at the loading docks to take you back to a moon. Maybe there, you can find a decent male to marry. One who is not a wanted fugitive by the Federation." Nova shook her head as she hissed. "I can't believe you got married. Stupid. Stupid."

Nue was used to her sister talking to her like she was an idiot. She was familiar with her sister popping into her life and telling her what to do.

But she was done taking orders.

However, fighting it out over a Minky call was not the answer. It would never end. So, she didn't say a word.

"Ready for the number?"

"Yes," Nue lied, though she would likely remember it anyway. At least long enough to placate her sibling.

"Good," Nova said before rattling off the Federation ID. As soon as she was done, she told Nue, "Now, repeat it back to me."

She did.

"Good, baby sister. Now leave the pad and get the hell off

that ship. I will be watching, and I will know if you don't listen to me."

"All right. I'll go."

"I know it's tough, but it's better to be alive than dead."

No, it wasn't. Because Nue would be alive, but her heart would be broken. If she left Rannn, she would be a traitor. A coward. But if she stayed on the ship by his side and died, at least she would die knowing that she was with the husband she loved.

And there was no doubt in her mind that she loved Rannn. Nue wasn't giving him up.

Not now.

Not ever.

"Will I see you after Marnak?" she asked, knowing the answer.

Nova shook her head. "No, I have things to do."

Nue nodded. Her sister had just proven her point. Nova was willing to save her, but there was a lack of familial love in the act.

"I understand," Nue said. Because she really did.

"All right, time's up. Bye, NoobyNue."

"Bye."

The call ended, and Nue set the Minky pad down. Then she slipped on her shoes and walked out of the cabin, hoping that Rannn wouldn't be mad at her for what she was about to do.

INSTEAD OF TAKING the elevator to the bridge, she turned to take the stairs. She wanted to rehearse how she was going to confess to Rannn what her sister had told her. She hoped he would take her warning seriously, especially if the Bolarks planned to remove him and/or kill him.

As she stepped into the stairwell, she heard a male say, "We can't trust them. We need to take them out now."

"You can't assume they're all bad. Arresting all of them out of fear is wrong," another male said.

"Are you not hearing me? I'm not asking if you want to, I'm *telling* you what you will do."

"I'm not going up there."

"Yes, you are."

Nue looked up and thought about rushing upstairs to tell Rannn that two guys were ready to storm the bridge and arrest him. But first, she needed to see who these guys were so she could describe them to her husband.

Creeping down the steps, she peered down and saw two Yunkin mutants. Surprised, she withdrew, expecting to see Bolarks.

Were the Bolarks looking to take down the Yunkins?

But if these were Yunkins and not Bolarks, who were they after?

Looking carefully, she noticed that one had horns on his forehead, and the other male had been talking to Rannn earlier. When she'd met him earlier, he didn't have any Night Demon manifestations. But now, his nails were long claws.

"Captain Rannn is up there. If I go in there, he will stop me."

"Not when I tell him that the Bolarks plan to kill us," Horns said.

"You don't know that."

"I told you, I got a message from my brothers on the planet. The Bolarks are taking over and killing anyone who looks at them the wrong way."

Nue swallowed. What her sister had told her was true. It was almost surreal to think of something so wild happening. To think that the Federation was dissolving so quickly with the Yunkins' demise.

It was just so insane.

"You say that, but how could they even do that? There are not enough Bolarks on Yunkin to begin with," Claws said.

"Spacestation Pegna is run by a Bolark and filled with Bolarks. My brother told me they sent down reinforcements."

Claws went to touch his neck, cut himself, and hissed. Looking at his own blood, he frowned.

"You have to face the facts, Oz. We're at war, and we need to take out the ones that would sabotage us from the inside."

Claws—Oz—didn't move, but Nue could see his resolve fading. "Captain Rannn trusts him. So should we."

Horns hit the wall with a fist. "Rannn is the reason behind all this. Think about it. Who could do this but a Numan? And Rannn's been going after them like they are on a hot- sheet. But this one they are talking about, Calum, he's the worst kind. The kind that creates diseases. Doesn't take a genius to figure out that instead of just going after Rannn, he went after our whole race. Not to mention, he wouldn't even tell his stupid doctor to remove these...*things*." The Yunkin grabbed one of his horns. "Rannn has lost his honor. You have to see that."

Oz shook his head as if he didn't know what the other male was talking about.

"Wow, you're just blind. Tell me, Oz, how many other Yunkin commanders do you see on this ship? None. Rannn surrounds himself with vile reprobates. His most trusted are a Yunkin-Red Demon hybrid, a full-blown Red Demon, a female Bolark, who doesn't know her place, a Numan, a bloody Outworlder, and oh, wait....more *Demons*."

"I talked to him earlier, and he didn't seem so bad."

"Yeah, well, he was probably faking. You're gullible," sneered Horns.

Oz lowered his head, and Nue realized she'd had enough. Filled with rage, she stomped down the last few steps so they could hear her. From the landing above where they were, she hissed out, "You know I used to hate all Yunkins because I've met more like you,"—she pointed to the horned mutant—"than you,"—she pointed to Oz. "And, to be honest, I don't like either one very much. Because that just means half your race is a bunch of backstabbing bastards, and the others are spineless cowards."

The bully mutant pulled out a phaser and pointed it right at her chest. It was in that moment that she realized she might have miscalculated her approach.

"Say another word, and I will shoot you. We are at the beginning of a war, and by the time anyone has time to remember to look for you, you'll be dead."

Nue thought about backing down and apologizing. But her contempt couldn't be silenced. "Said the honorable Yunkin who vowed to serve and protect."

"Don't you dare. I wasn't eavesdropping on a private conversation."

"Was it a conversation? It sounded more like mutiny."

"Rannn will pay for what he's done to us all," Horns said.

"The fact that you doubt him shows just how stupid you are. The safest place for you to be is on this ship, following his command."

"Like that worked out for his last crew. Just in case you didn't know, they all died."

She remembered Rannn talking about his previous crew. She remembered the remorse and guilt in his tone. She hated this Yunkin for what he was saying. Hated that he was the epitome of everything she loathed in the Yunkin race. Which was probably why she said, "It wasn't Rannn who caused this. It could have been Seth of Stars. He's punishing you for the monsters you've become. Just think about it. The ones who have more honor have retractable mutations. Those of you who are without honor, can't hide the depths of your depravity."

"How *dare you?*" he spat, and she saw a flash of light.

Her lungs seized, and her whole body braced for the pain. A *wopple* of air passed her ear, and it took a few seconds for her to realize what she was seeing.

Her knees lost their strength, and she hit the metal platform with a bang. Grey blood dripped from the belly of the horned Yunkin. His mouth was open, and blood dripped from there, too.

Oz's hand was embedded in the male's torso.

When Oz withdrew, he had something squishy in his palm. The other male flopped back, hitting the wall and slipping to the ground. His eyes were open, yet there was no awareness.

Oz dropped the squishy organ and turned to Nue. "I think you're right. I think Seth is punishing us." When Oz looked at his hand, Nue wondered if he would come after her or run away.

He did neither.

When he looked at her again, he said, "We need to go talk with the captain."

"Okay," she said. But after looking at the body, she asked, "What should we do about him?"

"Leave him for now." Oz slowly walked up the stairs, wiping off the blood. When he reached the platform, Nue stepped back, leery, wondering if he would attack her. His voice was soft when he said, "I'm not going to hurt you. You're Rannn's wife, and it is my duty to protect you."

Okay...

Oz led the way to the bridge. When they walked in, Rannn turned around with a look of impatience. Then he saw Oz and frowned. When Rannn noticed her, he whipped out of the seat. "What the hell happened?"

"Sir, I've come to inform you that there are traitors on this ship."

Rannn cut his eyes to Oz for a second as if willing him to shut up.

Nue felt his hands on her face and down her arms as if looking for a wound.

"Sir, Officer Wohl told the rest of the Yunkins that the Bolarks are seizing power in the Federation. He told us that they are coming to kill us, too."

"I know."

Oz was contemplative for a moment. "They sent me to arrest Sol for being a traitor to the Federation."

"Me?" Sol said from the helm. "What did I do?"

"I knew something was fishy about you," Clalls said, tapping his chin mockingly.

"Shut up, Clalls," Rannn said, letting Nue's arms go. "What happened?" Rannn said, ignoring everyone else and focusing solely on her. She felt like the queen of the universe at that moment. All the chaos currently in motion, and he made *her* a priority.

"Nova called me from the Minky pad you gave me. She told me the Bolarks are coming after you. She gave me a Federation ID to use on the lifepod to escape the upcoming battle. She said they have orders to remove all Yunkins from duty."

Something washed over his face. Something that looked like pride, though she wasn't sure.

"And you came to warn me?"

"I'm your wife. I'm not leaving you."

His nostrils flared, and she saw the raw emotions on his face for a microsecond. In a whisper so low she could barely hear, he said, "My wife trusts me."

She nodded. He grabbed her head and pulled her forehead to his lips for a hard kiss. When he let go, he said, "My wife is also a navigator."

She smiled, feeling a burn in her chest, pride that her husband needed her help. "What can I do for you?"

"Find a spot for the Garna that is off the Federation maps. We need to make it hard for the armada to find us."

"Easy," she said and walked to the navigation spot next to Clalls.

"Do you think you can create a unique path for forty-six other ships?" Rannn asked from his captain's chair.

"Do you have the coordinates of those ships?"

"Sol," Rannn called out, "give her the coordinates of the ships."

"Yes, sir," Sol said and began typing on his screen.

Nue glanced at the navigation station and tapped the screen, feeling more confident on the bridge than she ever had before.

Behind her, she heard Rannn tell Oz, "I assume there's a preparation meet-up for the rest of the Yunkins."

"Yes, sir."

"Good, take me there."

She watched him leave. She knew he was a warrior, but still, she worried.

25

MUTINY

The moment Rannn stepped into the elevator with Oz, he said, "It's hard to believe you and my wife just happened to be entering the bridge at the same time. What happened?"

Oz swallowed. "She caught Officer Wohl—the guy from the sparring ring with the horns—and me arguing about arresting Sol. Your wife stepped out of the shadow of the stairwell when Wohl was talking dishonorably about you."

Rannn pushed the warmth from his chest. Now wasn't the time to get all mushy about his amazingly loyal wife. He would reward her later with hours, days, and years of pleasure.

Unfortunately, the pride he felt about her was seared to his soul. He couldn't push out the feeling.

Oh, well. He would work with it. Focusing on the boy, he asked, "Is that his blood on your hand?"

"Yes...he was going to shoot your wife for telling him that he was a dishonorable bastard and that Seth of Stars was the one punishing us."

Rannn didn't think his wife had meant that. But she was part Sennite, and knew how to get to the core of someone. He remembered the time she'd told him to go stare at the walls. That'd cut him deeply.

"Do you think Seth is punishing us?" Oz asked instead of voicing his opinion.

Thinking about it, Rannn saw Oz hit the button for level one. On the way down, he said, "No."

Rannn didn't need to turn to see that he had Oz's full attention. When he paused for too long, Oz asked, "Is it because you don't believe in Seth of Stars?"

Rannn looked down at Oz's hands, his nails that were no longer claws. He pointed to the blood-encrusted fingers. "I believe in Seth. Though when I was used as a fighting slave, I realized that Seth didn't favor Yunkins. They died just as easily as every other race. But every time I took a fight for another crewmember, just to spare him a day, Seth gave me strength to fight with honor."

The door dinged and readied to open, but Oz pressed his finger against the close button. "I don't understand."

"Seth only rewards acts of honor. Meaning, he helps those who are helping others or acting for the greater good."

Oz looked at his hands mournfully. "So, Seth doesn't favor Yunkins?"

"No, I don't think he does. I think he favors anyone who faces their fears instead of becoming a mutinous tarq." Rannn pointed at the close button. "Time to sort the honorable from the disgraceful. Starting with my crew."

RANNN WALKED INTO LEVEL ONE, which was mainly the engine room and storage for their extra weapons. A group of Yunkins gathered around Lizzard, who announced, "We have to act. If we take over this ship and take out the Bolark planet, they will remember that we are the Federation. We started it, and we will defend it."

"Actually," Rannn bellowed, causing every head to turn his way, "the Terrans started the Federation. But that's beside the point. By all means, continue with your plan."

Lizzard looked at Rannn and then Oz. "Come to kill us? Come to finish what you started when you made us all into these freaks?"

Rannn watched as some nodded in agreement. Others looked worried at being caught.

"We all know that a Numan did this. Maybe not Ansel, but the one you've been hunting."

Rannn silently raised his hand and beckoned the speaker forward with two fingers.

At first, he didn't move. But Rannn knew it was only a matter of time before he realized that the longer he hesitated, the weaker he appeared. Several moments later, the speaker stood before Rannn.

"When did honorable Yunkins turn into insubordinate children?" The young male frowned at the offense. Rannn didn't care. Hell, he didn't have time for this crap at all. Scanning the crowd, he said, "For those of you who happened to lose your way and ended up here accidentally, I suggest you leave now and man your posts. An armada is headed this way, and I need my gunners in place."

Several moved towards the elevator, but no one left.

Looking back at the idiot, Rannn said, "And for those of you who want to take over the ship, I'm right here. Let's get this over with."

Backing up, Rannn bent his knees and squared his shoulders. His Night Demon mutation sprouted from his arms and knuckles seconds later.

Lizzard looked behind him, and Rannn counted three others

that seemed to plan on joining. Pity. The idiot would need a lot more than that.

Lizzard threw the first punch, telegraphing it so badly that Rannn grabbed the male's fist, twisted hard, and used his other hand to dislocate the tarq's elbow. Then he dropped down and used the momentum of the fall to break his shoulder joint.

Screams echoed off the metal walls in blood-curdling resonance. The second fighter tried to kick Rannn in the face, but he rolled, and the hit missed. The third and fourth mutants hesitated to come forward, leaving the second fighter an easy mark.

He twisted back with a swift roll of his hips, grabbed an ankle, and used his horned forearm to crunch through the second male's knee.

Another high-pitched scream that Rannn put out of his mind because they were alive, just in pain.

When he stood, he noticed a huddle of females near the elevator, all of them stunned. The males were still spread out, but they all seemed afraid.

"I don't know where your honor went, or if you ever had it to begin with, but you better find it now—or borrow it, for Seth's sake. There is only one Bolark on this ship, and I trust him. I trust every Terran. Honestly, I would trust any other race but you cowards. You want to moan about your Demon features, do so, but do it when we're not in the middle of a battle. Now, get back to your posts and do your damn jobs."

Rannn looked at Oz and then jerked his chin. "Come, I'm going to need another spokesperson for the next part of my plan."

26

POWER PLAY

Rannn didn't waste time as he walked into the bridge. "Clalls, did you connect to those captains?"

"Yes, I did. And they are on their way."

"Good. Will any of the ships get here in time, Nue?"

"Ten will get here before the armada arrives. Seventeen are too far away and won't get to the rendezvous spot for another seventy-two hours," Nue said, perched on the navigator seat. Rannn liked her there. Not because she looked like a proper Federation worker, but because he wanted her close.

If they were going into a firefight, he preferred for her to be in his cabin. But having her near gave him instant knowledge of whether or not she was okay.

"All right, sounds good." To Clalls, Rannn said, "Hail Armsono and make sure it's a video call and that he can only see me and Oz."

Clalls began typing on his communication screen. Within minutes, he reached back and pointed at Rannn. "It's connecting in three...two...one."

The captain's Minky screen went from black to a pale background and then focused on Admiral Armsono sitting at a

Minky desk. "Rannn, how convenient that you called. Although I'm not sure how, since the quantum network is down."

The Bolark unwrapped a little red cube and popped it into his mouth, then leaned back and arrogantly crossed his arms over his chest. "So, what can I do for you?"

"Considering that you're on a direct path to my ship, why don't you tell me what *you* want."

Armsono leaned forward smugly. "I see you aren't showing any signs of the disease. I assume your Numan shaved off the bone mutations because you think that if you don't look diseased, I won't remove you from your position. You're wrong. The disease eats away at a Yunkin's mind until they go crazy."

"I'm not crazy. I have two Numans on my ship. Had I showed signs of mental degeneration, they would have told me so. But if you're referring to this," he said, letting the spiked bones slip out of his skin, feeling the sting, "that's a different thing altogether."

"You shouldn't have two Numans on board. You probably had them alter the mutation of your arm to make you look more in control. But I know better. I saw what this disease did to the citizens of Yunkin," Armsono said, flinging his hand towards the screen.

Rannn took in several slow, deep breaths to calm his heart and emotions, and his arms smoothed out again. "The virus did alter me. But it has not controlled me. Federation law states that a doctor must evaluate a person's insanity and sign off on it before they can be removed from office. I see no report, and I will not step down."

"When millions of Federation Yunkins riot against their rules, I don't need to have a doctor's analysis for each and every person to do my job."

"How convenient that you think you can change the laws to fit your agenda."

Armsono snarled. "The only agenda I have is to serve and protect."

"Really? And how does riding front seat in an armada flight help you achieve that? Because from here, it looks like you're readying to attack."

Tapping the table, Armsono said, "See. You're already showing signs of paranoia."

"Just calling it as I see it."

"Or a Cerebral has taken over your mind." Armsono smiled as if he had finally trapped Rannn. "Both those Outworlders should be seized and killed. They are a hazard to our way of life."

"You're an idiot, Armsono. I've seen sniveling bastards like you climb the ranks before, but I will never understand how you made council admiral. I've proven myself over and over, and so has every single member of my crew. And you still have it out for them. That's not honor, that's corruption."

Armsono began to chuckle. "Jealousy is a nasty habit that all Yunkins suffer from."

Lies.

Rannn thought he might be able to reason with the idiot, but he was determined. And people motivated by fear were the worst.

Soberly, he addressed the Bolark. "My ship is not diseased, and I am not unfit to lead." Rannn nodded at Oz, who had been able to hide the claws. "And I am not the only one who can control the virus's mutation."

Oz's claws were instantly in the air.

Armsono didn't look convinced, but Rannn nodded to the boy again. Slowly, the claws retracted.

"This is what happens when we control ourselves. When we...act with honor."

Slapping his hand on the table, Armsono said, "If you think I will fall for this Numan trick, you don't know me very well. This is over. You are done. I have evidence that the disease will corrupt your mind in addition to your body. So, you *will* step down when I arrive. Or I will make you."

"You have no authority to do so," Rannn challenged.

"I'm your superior. I absolutely *do* have the authority. Consider this your trial."

"You would have to be the head council admiral to be my judge and jury."

Armsono opened his arms wide. "Exactly. Admiral Hobath is dead. I'm the most senior member of the admiral council. Therefore, I am, by default, Federation leader. Now...do you get it? You have a little over four hours before I arrive. For your crew's sake, I suggest you and the other diseased members be in cuffs and in the brig when I do. Anywhere else, and I'll consider it an act of aggression and shoot first. Because I know firsthand how beastly your kind can get with the brain disease."

Armsono stood up from his desk and signaled to someone. When he looked back at the screen, he said, "Goodbye, Rannn. I look forward to seeing what you decide to do."

The call terminated, and Oz immediately rubbed his head. "If he's head council admiral, then he has the right to discharge all of us."

Rannn ignored that trash and looked at Clalls. "Everything went through? They all heard?"

"Loud and clear."

TEN MINUTES before the armada was within range to start attacking, Yon and the crew were thirty minutes out of range. The other ships would arrive soon, but that didn't calm him. Rannn sat in the captain's chair, knowing that his crew was at the ready.

The air had a chill to it, and the silence made the bridge uninviting.

His beautiful wife kept looking at him with such confidence, he was practically buzzing with the desire to take her back to their cabin and love her for hours.

Clalls sat drinking a Niffy, staring at his screen as if he were about to fall asleep.

Oz chewed on his claws. If the boy still had nails full-time, they would be nubs by now.

Sol kept alternating between scratching and rubbing parts of his head and neck. The Bolark stood up and pointed down at his screen. "Sir...there are even more ships now. There have to be thousands."

Rannn could understand the male's fears. Thousands were a lot of ships, and if this came down to one ship pitted against all those, their chances of survival weren't good.

Rannn had bought time by flying in uncharted territory. Still, the armada had only slowed down enough to change course and follow. They were now in a dark part of space with no other planets or anything for millions of light years. It was as good a place as any to have a battle.

Clalls yawned before saying, "Armsono is hailing you. Are you up for a chat?"

Rannn grabbed the arms of his seat, ready to stand, when he had a devilish idea. "Clalls? I'm supposed to be in chains, remember. Want to play captain for a few minutes?"

The Demon's voice was almost a reverent whisper. "Yes." Then he cleared his throat, and Rannn could see the change on his face. The male stood up and snapped his fingers at Rannn. "You're in my seat, boy. Move."

Rannn mumbled, "I'm already regretting this," as he stood up with a growing smile. To Oz, he jerked his chin and mouthed, *let's go*. As he left the bridge, he was surprised that he heard every word of the call on the ship's speakers.

Armsono's voice. "Clalls? What the hell are you doing? Where's Rannn?"

"Hello, Armsono. You may address me as *Captain*."

"I will not. Now, tell me where Rannn is, or I will have you on a ship to Debsa before you can blink."

Rannn had just stepped into the elevator as Clalls said, "Really? That's your threat? Do you have any idea how many Federation guards owe me favors? And most of them work on Debsa. I'd live like a king."

Oz, who stood next to Rannn, whispered, "Do you think he's telling the truth?"

"Yes, I do."

Armsono's voice reached an unusually high octave when he screeched, "You lie. My cousin runs Debsa, and he's an honorable Bolark."

Clalls chuckled. "Chez has the brainpower of a gnat. He ignores everything that's happening on the planet because he spends all his time inside his hangar with a harem of over three hundred males and females. He likes to be spanked whilst being told he's a bad boy."

Beside Rannn, Oz made a sound as if he were going to vomit. Rannn was about to tell him it was probably a lie, but then Clalls added, "The Red Demon who really runs Debsa is actually an inmate named Demire. There are no official Federation security guards left on the planet. But...given you're the head councilor, I figured you already knew that. Although, I can't say it looks good for your reputation to have a prisoner-run prison planet."

"Chez would never. And I know you're lying. All you Demons do is lie. It's why your race should never have been allowed to join the Federation. You should all be locked up on a planet far away and left to die," Armsono hissed.

"Funny you say that," Clalls said with a hint of something truly sinister in his voice. "Because according to my research, eleven Bolarks went missing. And all eleven were higher-ranking than you. Coincidental that a week after their disappearance, you assumed your current position. I have found seven of the eleven on various moons and other inhabitable planets."

"You can't accuse me of their disappearance. And even if you did find these people, you can't blame me for their deaths."

"Not all died. One survived. Do you remember Captain Argat?"

Rannn didn't have to see the screen to know that the gasp he heard was from Armsono.

The elevator pinged, and both he and Oz walked out into the docking bay. Along the sides lay some of the ship's railguns and cannons. As he passed his Weapons and Tactical guards, he nodded to them and made sure to pat each one on the shoulder.

Rannn stepped up to an empty cannon and pointed to the next one down the way. "Grab a spot, Oz, and get ready."

The conversation between Clalls and Armsono had stopped, and Rannn assumed that Clalls had done exactly what he had hoped he'd do. A moment later, the ship's lights dimmed for a pulse. Then red lights blinked, and the alarms sounded.

The one-hundred-and-eighty-degree screen showed the incoming hostile ships. Rannn sat down, adjusted his feet, and grabbed the handles. Then he spun and began shooting at the sloops that fired on the Garna. The many thousands of shots from the sloops sounded like someone pounding into the hull with an industrial-sized sledgehammer.

The high-pitched whine of the Garna's railgun was heard before it released four shots. The blast vibrated the ship.

Rannn prayed to Seth of Stars that he had planned accordingly and that his crew would not see their deaths.

With each shot, Rannn zoned out, working on autopilot, shooting down as many ships as he could to preserve his crew. The guns, cannons, drills, and railguns burst and blasted. It was as if Garna herself knew that she was fighting for her life.

The more Rannn shot down, the more sloops took their place. For every one he tagged, five more rushed by, taking shots at the ship—particularly at the belly where they were the most vulnerable. It was a flawed design that Rannn had determined just by looking. If any of those pilots were even half-decent, they would know, too.

The screen was thick with ships, and Rannn didn't see an easy win. Hell, he was looking at a fight that he was supposed to lose. His memories took him back to the cages of Angny, where he'd fought for his life every day.

A cold shiver ran up his spine.

Death was creeping nearer, trying to whisper a soft melody in his ear, lying to him that everything would be better once he was asleep.

Gritting his teeth, he kept shooting, not bothering to think about life or death, winning or losing. All that mattered was looking for the next target. He needed to keep going. Nothing would stop him. Death might take him, but until then, he would never stop fighting.

The ship's light started to blink purple. That meant they had sustained extensive damage. It was a warning to leave the level or risk being sucked into space when the hull was fully breached.

The two cyborgs nearest Rannn looked his way. He bellowed, "Leave." One got up, but when he noticed that no one else was vacating, he sat back down and remained at his position.

The fight continued, and the lights turned black. Rannn heard a plunk and then a whoosh as all the air moved quickly. The hull had been breached somewhere behind him, and space was currently sucking everything and everyone out.

He could hear screams. In another ten seconds, the air leveled out and re-pressurized, and Rannn knew the crew had done what protocol demanded and sealed off this section of the bay. It wasn't a win, but he was still damn proud of his team for taking care of it so fast.

The guards continued taking down the attackers. Minutes later, the lights blinked black again. This time, the breach was closer to Rannn. He was ripped from his seat, and just barely able to grab hold of the next cannon. The cyborg manning the position held on, too, her face steeled and without fear.

Seconds later, the suction was gone, and the cyborg moved back to her seat to resume her duty. Rannn did the same, but then...all the ships stopped firing. Suddenly, some of them began to wobble before carelessly flying into another vessel.

Chollar.

I'm here.

Finally.

I leave for a few days and look what you get yourself into.

Rannn tried not to smile as he watched thousands of ships crashing into one another. So many lives lost because of a nasty admiral on a power trip.

The ships stopped blowing up. Instead, they just remained stationary with a slow drift. Chollar must have heard his thoughts.

Thank you.

I just put them all to sleep. It's actually easier this way.

Just then, the lights in the bay blinked yellow, indicating an incoming spacecraft. Considering the damage, he hoped the pressurized section would hold. Moving from his cannon, he walked to the receiving area. Instead of Sasha's ship incoming, he saw five galleon ships.

Who the hell was this?

Something you should see, Chollar said into his mind.

As the ships opened, all of the Weapons and Tactical guards filed in behind him. Oz stood to Rannn's right and the cyborg female to his left. All five ships lowered their ramps. Then, from each one, a handful of Bolarks walked out and directly to him.

When Rannn saw the vile hatred in their eyes, he suspected they weren't standing before him because they wanted to.

One tried to talk, but all that came out was a mindless growl. Then, they all hit their knees at the same time and subsequently fell on their faces, unconscious.

"What just happened?" Oz said.

Chollar happened, but Rannn wasn't going to say that.

Rannn pointed to the ships. "Go find out who's in those ships," he said, having a gut feeling about who was inside. He just hoped that they weren't all dead.

Oz's face was dark grey when he came out alone. His eyes burned with tears, and Rannn had his answer.

"They shot them. They shot hundreds of Yunkins. Not all of them were Federation, either."

Rannn didn't say a word. Instead, he felt the bony protrusions in his arms and knuckles. Part of him wanted them to stand trial for their crimes. The other part couldn't wait that long to exact vengeance.

In one move, Rannn took his fist and smashed it down on one of the unconscious Bolark's neck, severing the head from the body in one move. The death felt hollow but seemed necessary.

The Yunkin hybrids from his crew executed the rest, their faces drawn and solemn. Rannn took in his crew that had manned the ship's weapons and memorized their faces. "You didn't give up or run away when losing was almost inevitable."

The crew stared at him from where they stood or sat, a look of a painful victory on their faces.

"You fought with honor. And I couldn't be prouder. This,"—he pointed to the dead Bolarks—"is why we became Federation. To stop the senseless slaughter of the masses. We vowed to serve and protect. Some of you might have forgotten that, but I hope this burns into your minds so you never forget again. Seth rewards the honorable, regardless of skin color."

The air was foul with blood and silence. Rannn assumed that they had heard enough. Just as he was turning to leave, he heard Clalls over the ship's speaker system.

"Co-Captain Rannn, please return to the bridge. I have to pee, and I refuse to leave the infant to handle the bridge."

And just like that, snickers abounded.

"Oh, and bring a case of Niffys," Clalls instructed.

Rannn shook his head. He was never going to hear the end of this.

INSIDE THE BRIDGE, Clalls frowned. "Where are my Niffys?"

Rannn ignored Clalls and walked directly to Nue, who had a new scratch on her face. The station that would have been the navigation area flickered and looked a bit smashed. She must have been rocked into it during the fight.

His stomach squeezed.

"It's okay, it doesn't hurt." She winced as he grazed the swollen part of her eye.

He didn't have words, but he did feel the need to pull her into his arms, careful with his extra bones as he held her. Pressing his mouth to her head, he kissed her.

Minutes later, he felt the tension drain from his body, and the bones receded from his arms and knuckles.

"I get that you're newly mated and all that, but you have a video call," Clalls said from the captain's chair. He still lounged in it with one leg dangling over the arm.

"From who?"

"The last remaining council admiral. But you know...keep 'em waiting. They like that."

Rannn felt Nue tense. She looked up at him, clearly worried. "What do you think they are going to say?"

Honestly, he didn't care. They could fire him, and he would be fine because he wouldn't lose her. He kissed her head again and told her, "I'm sure they will want a recounting of everything."

It was then that Rannn looked past his wife to Sol, who sat near the trash shoot, looking sickly. "You okay, Sol?"

The Bolark looked up and shook his head. "We almost died. So many ships. So much damage. Ten spacecrafts that came to help us were blown up. All those people are now dead. *Dead.* We should be dead, too. The ship is broken." Sol jerked once from his belly, then scrambled up and vomited into the trash shoot with little to nothing coming out.

Rannn pulled Nue tighter against him, thinking about what Sol had said. They *should* be dead. But they weren't.

His heart began thumping at the prospect of what was to come. But he tried to remain calm so he could hold his wife a little longer.

She pressed a kiss to his chest and whispered, "I love you," loud enough for only him to hear.

His arm spikes came out as he felt pressure in his chest. His need for his wife. The desire to repeat those words while he was inside her. "I love you, too."

27

COUNCIL

"I wish the screen was turned around. I would have loved to see Rannn tell his female that he loved her. I never knew he was such a romantic," said a female voice from the captain's Minky screen.

Rannn turned to Clalls and glared at the Demon for putting the call through without him being ready. "You could have waited until I was done," he said.

Clalls made a face. "Actually, I've had them patched into the video call from the first time you talked to Admiral Armsono. Well, actually, I had all the ships not in the armada patched in. Plus all the planet admirals and the council admirals. So, you know....no one could say they didn't get an invite to the party and inevitably feel left out."

Rannn would never doubt Clalls' shrewdness ever again.

Nue patted his chest and went to take a seat. He thought about bringing her with him to show her off, but Nue was not that kind of female. She didn't need to be seen. She just wanted to be with him.

It was a profound feeling, and he could bask in that truth for the rest of his life.

Stepping in front of the screen, Rannn saw five council admirals. Notably missing was Orin, his cousin. His heart dropped.

The Hetten female was the first to speak. "I'm council admiral Devika." Holding her hand out, she pointed to the others next to her and introduced the male Krant as Admiral Dern. He'd been the judge over his trial when Rannn had accused Armsono of neglecting Eldon.

A male Grach, a female Terran, and a female Sennite were also there, but Rannn didn't catch their names.

"We heard about everything Armsono has done. As of this moment, he is discharged from his service in the Federation, and his record will state that he has been found grossly dishonorable."

Rannn didn't comment or nod because as they were talking about Armsono's record, he wondered if the bastard was dead.

"Yes. Very dead," Chollar answered telepathically.

"Do you have anything else you wish to add about Armsono's actions?" Devika asked.

"No."

"The archives will reflect our ruling." When Rannn didn't say anything, the Hetten said, "I'm aggrieved by the deaths that Armsono has caused. While we all thought we were sheltering in place, he was laying claim to the Federation. We will not be fooled so easily again."

Rannn thought that was a clever way of bowing out and not taking responsibility for their fellow admiral's actions.

Devika looked at her fellow admirals before stating, "Clalls sent us the final disclosure from Commander Ansel about this mutation. According to him, it will not eat away at your mind and make you mindless. The mutation affects bone growth and remodeling, and enlarges the amygdala, the part of the brain that influences pleasure, aggression, and anger. In other words, it looks more like Demon physiology compared to Yunkin, but it is not something that will cause all Yunkins to lose their minds."

Rannn tilted his head, waiting for the admiral to get to the point.

"We have agreed, and will record our unanimous agreement, that the Yunkin race is not in danger of becoming mindless savages. They are not prohibited from active duty. So long as they can act honorably and responsibly."

Rannn inhaled and exhaled loudly. Something he probably wouldn't have done before, but there was no reason *not* to show the council that they were wasting his time. What he wanted to know was what they planned to do about the Bolark revolt.

Devika eyed him for a moment, giving a silent reprimand. Rannn responded by sitting down and opening his arms, silently reprimanding her for wasting his bloody time.

The Krant admiral snorted. "You know, Devika, I've been Captain Rannn's judge before. To be honest, I don't think the disease has changed anything about him. He's just as blunt and ornery as before."

"Respectfully," Rannn said, sitting forward, "I'd like you to get to the point. I have a ship that needs to be repaired, and several other ships that may need my assistance. Especially those who took their Yunkins or stuffed them into their brigs. They are out there suffering right now, and the longer I sit here waiting for whatever you're going to say about what will be done about this coup, the more chance that people will die."

Admiral Dern held up his large, yellow hand. "What would you do if you were admiral and had to clean up this mess?"

Rannn narrowed his eyes.

Dern smirked.

"I'm merely a captain." And if that bastard thought to promote him, he would not take it. He wasn't giving the rest of his life to the Federation.

"Who took on an armada and won," Dern said. "That's not something just any captain could do."

"I have a big ship. And I didn't do anything by myself. My crew fought honorably."

"You're an excellent leader. Unorthodox at times, but extremely effective. So, I ask you again. What would you do if you had to decide everyone's fate?"

Rannn could feel the eyes of everyone on screen and everyone on the bridge. He also knew that this trial, if that was even what it was, was being broadcasted across the Federation.

"Disciplinary actions need to be taken against every person serving in the armada. Even if they didn't do anything, they also didn't stand up and protect each other. That is the difference between acting with honor and being disgraceful."

Dern smirk fell to a nod of agreement. "What else?"

"Make a note that the battle was ended by one male, a Master Elder Cerebral named Chollar. To add to that, I think the Federation needs to become acquainted with the Outworlders so we can establish peace. They have abilities that we shouldn't be afraid of. They should be admired. We can co-exist."

"Consider your remarks noted."

"I'm not finished," Rannn said. "I also want every single Bolark that took a Yunkin life to apologize to the victims' families and let *them* decide their fate. I don't know the lengths of devastation that happened on Yunkin. Still, I am positive it will reverberate for hundreds of years to come. And even though you five were safe, did you take even a moment to think about the others? Not one Yunkin stands before you. Is that because you agreed with Armsono? You let him hide you for fear of the disease? Or did you agree with him and only now realize your error?"

Rannn could feel that his arms had visible mutations again.

His chest constricted at the idea that the five in front of him had been cowards.

Devika cut her eyes to the Krant.

Dern held his hand up to stop Devika from talking. "You know what I admire about you, Rannn? You don't respect rank. You expect a person to act honorably regardless of if he or she is a FAVI or an admiral. So, I'm not offended that you assumed I was hiding in some hole. But we were not hiding. We were locked down here. A Rana freed us and handed us a Minky pad, just in time to hear your conversation with Armsono."

Rannn almost looked at Clalls to tell him he'd done a damn fine job, but...being a Night Demon, he might misinterpret it as gratitude. Rannn didn't want to owe the male a favor later.

"Between the first call and the second, we had time to see what'd happened. I already contacted my planet to bring supplies and to help rebuild what was destroyed." The Krant took out an admiral seal from his pocket and held it up. "Yunkin will mourn their loss, but they will rebuild quickly. My word as admiral, I will do all I can to help."

Rannn was grateful to know that his planet wasn't being left to rot because of the mutation. He was also pleased that the admiral had made it personal by requesting help from his home planet.

Devika held up her admiral seal. "Help is on its way from Hetten, as well."

The others held up their seals and said the same thing for each of their planets.

Rannn nodded, almost offering a thank you and claiming the voice of his race. But he didn't, because he wasn't the voice. He wasn't an admiral.

"Rannn," Devika said. Rannn didn't like the sound of that.

Standing tall, he prayed to Seth that they weren't about to do what he thought they were.

"Rannn, you have been found worthy to stand as the voice of your people. As head council admiral following Armsono's death, I call you to the position of admiral lower-end."

Every part of him tensed. He didn't want this at all. "I don't want to be an admiral. Respectfully."

A blond brow rose. "I wasn't asking. It's your duty to accept this charge. Unless you're resigning altogether. Is that what you're doing?"

No, it was not what he was doing. Through clenched teeth, he said, "I accept my new position of admiral."

"Good," she said with a bit too much pep.

"Where will I be stationed?" he asked, needing to know if he was about to be the new admiral of Yunkin. If so, he'd need to drink bottles of Jubriaan before getting there.

"Space station Pegna needs a new crew and admiral to oversee it. The council and I have decided that Pegna should be relocated from outside Yunkin to the border between Federation space and the Outworlds. And as you put it earlier, we need to try and reach a peaceable understanding with them. I'm giving you the chance to be the liaison between us."

That...was a significant modification in Federation law.

"How much leeway do I have as liaison?"

"I'm sure you'll push for more than is necessary," she said with a smile and then added, "Plus, Orin will be thrilled that he doesn't have to plead your case anymore."

That sobered Rannn. "Is Orin alive?"

She nodded. "Very much so. He's just busy up top, helping to get food supplies and medical assistance to the people."

Rannn inhaled with relief.

Clalls stepped into the video and held up a finger. "As co-captain, does that mean I'm full captain now?"

The Hetten shook her head. "No. The councilors and I have discussed it, and we will be promoting Vivra to captain of the

Garna. I understand that she's on a mission, but she and I have been in contact before. She's perfect for the job."

Rannn liked that even more.

Clalls walked out of the video. "That's it, I'm retiring."

Devika pressed her hands together. "All right, Admiral Rannn, I think that's enough for today. I suspect that you and your crew have a lot to do. Goodbye."

Rannn repeated the farewell, and the call terminated. As soon as the screen was black, he asked Clalls, "Stop the feed."

Then he got up, grabbed his wife, and walked out of the bridge, needing her more than he needed air. He needed her to calm him, to keep him focused, and to rid himself of the black memories that'd bubbled to the surface. The ones that reminded him of how close and sweet death's lullaby had been.

28

SURPRISE

Nue woke with soreness from the hours of lovemaking after the battle. She reached over to the side of the bed and found it empty. Sitting up, she felt it again and noticed that it was cold.

Rannn had been gone for some time.

She gingerly rolled out of bed and took a hot shower. Looking at the mirror, she thought about the fact that she was staring at the fake her. The one that was supposed to be hiding from the Federation.

Touching her hair, she realized she didn't need to hide anymore. Sadly, she couldn't remove the black powder polymer from her hair. But she didn't need the metallic blue-grey contacts anymore.

Removing them, she saw her dark purple eyes for the first time in years. She'd almost forgotten the color.

Applying a bit of makeup and dressing in her non-Federation clothes—the one outfit she had—she left the cabin in hopes of finding her husband. If he was busy, she'd take a kiss and then eat breakfast alone.

If he wasn't...she just wanted to be with him.

She took the elevator to level six where the medical bay was located. Stepping out, she saw two guards standing outside the door. Oz was one of them. A cyborg, the other. When Oz saw her, he motioned for the others to let her pass.

"She's not Federation. She's not allowed past."

"She's the admiral's wife, you idiot," Oz hissed.

The guard didn't seem to think that was good enough, but he stepped back anyway. As she walked in, she suspected that she was only getting a kiss before eating alone.

Inside, Ansel and Penner peered down at a body in a medbed. Penner was the first to acknowledge her. "Hello. Are you in need of medical attention?"

"I was looking for Rannn." Nue scanned the room, not seeing him, but she saw the niskie curled into a ball, sleeping on Ansel's medical coat near the corner of the room.

Ansel finally looked up. "He's on the bridge, talking with Vivra. A captain-to-captain talk, I assume."

She thought about that and wondered if Rannn was upset to be leaving his ship. After the battle, he had been ferocious, not saying anything but how much he loved her.

At no time did he slow down and really talk to her.

As his wife, she felt like she should try and make time for them to talk and really get to know each other. Learn each other's hobbies and interests. Things like that.

"You took your contacts out. I like the purple better," Penner said, moving away from the bed.

She grabbed a piece of hair. "I would have gone back to my natural color, too, but it's..."

"Powder polymer, say no more. I can remove it."

"Really?"

"Of course. I'm a Numan, after all."

"How is that relevant?"

Penner grabbed something from a cabinet. "My sister was

the one who created powder polymer." Penner pressed a button on a white device that sounded like electricity zapping. "Here we are." When he got close enough, he took a piece of hair, typed it into the device, then pushed a button. All the black powder fell over her clothes and onto the floor.

"How did you do that?" she asked, amazed. Holding up her hands, she chuckled at first and then started laughing. "Is there a mirror somewhere?"

Penner took a Minky screen, turned on the video, and let her see her real face and hair. It was so different, she hardly recognized herself. In that moment, she looked at the dark powder covering her and the floor and worried that Rannn would think the same thing.

"Don't like the purple?" Penner asked.

"Not sure if Rannn will," she answered honestly.

"He's on his way back," Ansel said. "You won't have to wait long to find out." But then he stopped and observed her for several moments. "I like the purple better."

"Me, too," Penner said.

The niskie stretched and sniffed the air. Looking at her, the beast got up and trotted over. Nue moved to the side and hit a knee to pet the beautiful and terrifying creature. Honestly, there was something so pure about ugly beasts.

The medical door opened, and Nue saw Rannn walk in. He didn't even glance at her.

He pointed at the medbed. "Did the kid wake up?"

Ansel shook his head. "No, not yet. He's still coming out of his coma."

"Any viruses or sickness that could spread?"

Ansel shook his head again. "No."

"What have you learned about him from your machine?"

Ansel looked at Penner for a moment and then answered,

"He's a Numan hybrid. According to my scanners, he is nineteen."

"Numan like you, or like Calum? Do you think Calum cloned himself?"

"He's not a clone," Ansel said with a wince. "He's a Numan-Terran hybrid."

Rannn glanced in her direction and then looked back at Ansel. "If he's a—" He turned back to her and stared.

"Nue?"

She stood up and wiped her hands on her thighs. "Hi."

He looked her over like a male trying to get his bearings. As if he wasn't sure that he was looking at his wife. She wanted to slap herself for changing everything so fast. He clearly hated it. He hadn't even recognized her.

"Is something wrong?" He came closer and pulled her up to whisper, "Did I hurt you last night? I'll make sure to have a medscope in our room at all times."

"No. I just wanted to say hi and maybe see if you were free for breakfast. If not, then no worries."

"You're hungry, or you wanted to see me?"

She felt a blush overtake her face. Rannn's eyes darkened and the bones in his arms slowly rose to the surface.

"How long have you...? When did you change your hair?"

"Do you hate it? I can put it all back."

"Don't change anything."

She swallowed, knowing she was taking away from his captain time...no, his *admiral* time. "I'll let you do your thing."

His eyes darted to her lips.

"As if I'd let you eat alone."

She licked her lips, and his hand squeezed hers. "Wait with me until I'm done here?"

She'd wait with him forever. He was her husband, and she was determined to be a great wife.

A second later, he leaned down and whispered, "Over five hours of emptying myself inside you, and all I can think about is getting you back in my bed and hearing your moans in my ear."

Her face burned.

Being married to Rannn was not what she'd expected.

Rannn cleared his throat and turned to address Ansel. "When he wakes up, have Chollar question him and see how he ended up on Calum's ship. Maybe he will have a lead on where the tarq is."

The medical doors opened, and three people walked in: Chollar, his wife, Jandy, and Sci.

Rannn nodded. "Can you search the boy's memories and find out what happened to Calum? We need to find him."

"Of course, I can." Chollar then snapped his fingers and said, "Get up." Those words reverberated around Nue's mind. She could almost *feel* the command.

Ansel grunted before touching his head. A moment later, the medbed flashed red and then blue.

Nue watched as Chollar smiled. "Now I can hear." The Cerebral's yellow eyes darted to the side as if he were watching something no one else could see.

Sci tilted his head as if he were listening, too.

"Lock me in to what you're seeing?" Rannn said.

"That didn't work out well for you last time," Chollar said without looking.

"Do it," Rannn instructed. Nue instantly felt his hands slacken on hers.

Nue scanned the medical room and noticed that Penner looked confused, but Ansel stared off like he was watching the video, too. The two females that held their husbands' hands weren't paying attention to anything. They whispered about each other's hair.

Time ticked on for a few minutes before Rannn took a deep

breath. His grip tightened, and then he looked down at her. "Good news. The boy is not amoral."

"How do you know?" she asked.

"Chollar can search memories. All of them."

Oh.

She hadn't known that.

Ansel opened the medbed. The young boy inside sat up and looked around with wide eyes. "Who are you? Where's my mom?"

Ansel was the one to reply. "My name is Ansel. I'm a Federation doctor on Garna, the star carrier."

"What do you want?"

Ansel pointed at Chollar. "That is a Master Elder Cerebral. He was able to show us your memories so we knew what happened. We know you were kidnapped with your mother and used in a secret lab. We also know that the lab was run by a Numan named Calum. We also know that Calum is not your father."

The boy's mouth trembled. "How do you know?"

"Because I knew Calum. I know his DNA. And I checked."

"He wasn't my father? He said he was." The boy swallowed hard, then his eyes watered. He wiped them with his hand. "He was a monster. I hated him."

"We saw what he made you do."

The boy's watery eyes turned to full tears. "I didn't want to *hurt them!* He MADE ME."

"We know," Ansel said softly.

Nue felt her chest constrict from the pain in the boy's voice. It cracked as he sobbed. She wanted to go to him, but Rannn held her fast to his side.

"You did the right thing, Arvey. You did the right thing."

Arvey's hands were still on his face. "I couldn't let him kill them all."

Nue looked up at Rannn. Rannn's jaw tightened.

"You did the right thing," Ansel said again.

Sci stepped forward and flicked his hand, and the boy fell back in a slump, eyes closed and mouth open. Asleep. "Chollar. Remove the memories. No one deserves that."

Ten seconds later, Chollar said, "Done, brother."

Nue almost gasped. So, not only could Chollar search memories, he could also destroy them. Holy Seth, that was scary.

Penner looked at Ansel. "How did you know what the boy did?"

"Cerebrals are telepaths. Surely, you can understand what that means."

Penner rolled his eyes before asking, "What did Arvey do? What was the *right thing*?"

"Calum's disease was meant to wipe out all Yunkin purebloods. Arvey changed the virus and stopped Calum from committing genocide," Ansel answered.

"How?" Penner asked.

"By *stopping* Calum."

Penner tilted his head towards the boy. "He killed the Numan?" Penner's voice was a mixture of awe and disappointment.

"Yes. And then the ship tried to kill *him*. Apparently, Calum had some kind of safeguard chip that alerted the virus containers if he died."

"I don't understand. If the ship tried to kill Arvey, how did he escape? Also, how did he stop the virus that was going to kill all the Yunkins?" Penner asked.

"During the testing phase, Arvey took the virus and spliced it with Night Demon DNA to change the internal coding. So, when Calum loaded the pods with his disease, he didn't know it had been changed. Arvey didn't know that each pod was also filled with arsenice to kill the head of the planet and each captain. I assume Calum did that as a diversion so his virus could kill without anyone knowing until everyone was already dead."

"How did he escape?"

"He didn't. He stuffed himself inside a pod and destroyed the uplink system so the ship couldn't get to him. Until said ship responded to a proximity alert and attacked Chollar. Chollar ripped the whole thing apart, as one like him does."

Penner looked to Chollar as if he were trying to understand how a simple-looking male could do so much.

Nue didn't know how Chollar did it either, but she believed that he could. He was becoming more terrifying by the second. The male had *ripped* a ship apart? With his...brain parts? Why would Seth of Stars even create beings like that? Seriously.

Ansel announced, "I understand what Arvey did, and now I can cure the virus."

"Really?" Penner asked. "How long will it take to make enough of the cure?"

"With you, I can have it done in thirty-six hours."

Penner's chest rose. "It would be my pleasure."

The room fell silent for a moment, and Nue felt compelled to ask, "Everything will go back to normal? Bones and all?"

Because....she kind of liked them on Rannn.

She felt his hand squeeze hers. She was too embarrassed to look up.

"Everything will go back to normal." Ansel jerked his chin at Penner. "Come on. The faster we get this done, the quicker we can get out of here."

"You act like you have somewhere to be." Penner frowned.

"I do," Ansel said firmly. "This is my last mission. I'm leaving with Sci and going to the Outworlds after this."

Penner stopped. "Seriously?"

"Yes."

Penner turned around to look at Rannn. "You're just going to let him go? Look at how much good he does for you. What would you do without him?"

Rannn's voice was a little harsh. "He's my friend. I don't intend to stop him from retiring. He's earned it."

"Quitting," Ansel said back.

"Retiring," Rannn said firmly. "I wouldn't allow you to leave in any other way."

They stared at each other, and she could see the emotions on both their faces. Finally, Ansel said, "Retiring, then."

When Ansel and Penner were gone, Sci said, "Arvey is smart. He knows his mother is dead, but his mind was hurt with the trauma. He's going to need a family. Someone to look after him."

"What are you saying?" Rannn asked point-blank.

Nue cut Sci off from what he was about to say and asked, "You want us to take him? As in...adopt him?"

"He could have family back on Earth. We should look for them."

Chollar shook his head. "He has no idea who his mother is related to."

"Ansel could run a blood scan and see if anyone in the Federation pops up as a relative. It can't be that hard."

Nue didn't like this side of Rannn. Helping the recently orphaned boy was a good thing. An honorable thing. "I want to adopt him," she said in a firm voice.

Rannn looked down. "He's over the age to be adopted."

"I don't care."

He held her eyes for what felt like ages, and then he smiled. "How about we take him with us to Pegna. And instead of adopting him, we find him a medical mentor who can train him to be a doctor. He's smart. It wouldn't take much time to train him."

Nue kind of liked it, but she still felt like Rannn wasn't willing to take care of the boy the way a teenager who'd lost a parent needed to be looked after.

"Who would be his mentor?"

His brows pulled together. "You need a name right now?"

"I will look over their profile and see if they are a good fit."

Rannn let go of her and crossed his arms. "And how would you know if they are a good fit?"

"I'd know."

He held up his hands. "I don't know. Honestly, there isn't anyone..." He dropped his arms and then looked at the wall vacantly for a second. "My mother."

"Your mom?" Was that a good idea?

"Yes. She took Ansel under her wing and supported his genius. She could do the same for Arvey."

Nue wasn't too excited about Rannn's mom being on the same ship as them. What if she didn't like that Rannn was married to her? What if his mother tried to be all...*motherly* to Rannn. That was Nue's job, and she took it seriously.

"Should I take your silence as a tacit agreement?"

No. "Fine."

Rannn chuckled.

She didn't like it, but then again, it was better than Rannn being upset. She looked to the Cerebrals to change the subject, and was astonished to find the room empty aside from her, Rannn, and Orna.

"They left."

"Because I took over the topic?" she asked, worried that Rannn might take this moment to remind her that he wouldn't always obey her instructions.

"No, they went to breakfast. Ready to join them?"

Oh. "Um, before we go, can we talk about the cure?"

Rannn took her hand and pulled it up to his face. "I'm not taking it. Even if you're in favor of it, I won't do it. I like 'em."

She did, too. Grinning, she leaned in to him and confirmed it aloud. "Me, too."

He got that heated look in his eyes again. "Maybe we should skip breakfast."

Shaking her head, she said, "No way. I need food before you sex me to sleep for another four hours."

29

GOODBYES

Rannn sat at the head of a table in a private room in the galley. It was the last dinner he would have with his friends. His wife sat in his lap, and he couldn't stop looking and feeling her beautiful purple hair. It was silkier now than when it was black.

He loved it.

Yon had been watching him for a while, and Rannn wondered when the male would say whatever he wanted to say. Instead of saying anything, the male kissed his mate, who was in his lap too, before standing her up and making his way over.

Rannn stood up as well, ready.

Yon held out a black rong, a Yunkin device that all married males used to capture memories of their spouses when they were away. "I had one shipped a while back. Figured you might just make her your wife. Wanted to be prepared if you did."

Nue, who was standing by his side, snorted. "I don't know how you thought that by the way he treated me."

Rannn wished he could go back and kick himself in the balls for what he'd put her through. He also knew that she had not forgotten, and he hated that. Not that he expected her to. But he wanted her to think of him as her husband, not as the male he had been.

"Rannn never took his eyes off you. From the second he met you. Even after he found out about your past, it just gave him a reason to demand that you stay closer. You won't get it because you're not Yunkin. But I do. And I saw him claim you the moment Sasha introduced you."

Rannn was done with the conversation. Taking the rong, he shook hands with the male. "Thank you."

"Gift time!" Pax said excitedly. "You are going to love what we got you."

Rannn looked at the Red Demon and realized that this goodbye dinner was doubling as a wedding feast. And it looked like all his friends had brought him gifts. His throat ached for a moment at how much he would miss them.

Pax stood up and pulled out Vivra's chair. They reached behind the food stand and held up a wrapped box. Rannn shook his head. "Jubriaan?" he guessed.

"Half is Paranoise, an expensive wine that I trust Nue will love, because I assume she has better taste buds than yours for Demon brew," said Vivra. She handed the big box to Nue and then pulled out a smaller one. "And my gift to you."

Rannn watched as Nue opened the small box. Inside was a black-chained necklace with a round charm. It swirled around like there was something living inside it. Nue reached in and pulled out a black ring that matched. She tried to put it on her thumb, but it didn't fit. Rannn knew what it was. He took it from her and slipped it onto his finger. Instantly, he felt a small pulse.

He could feel her heartbeat.

She touched her necklace. "Oh, wow."

To Vivra, Rannn said, "Thank you."

Jandy and Sasha rose and handed over two more wrapped gifts. Rannn signaled for them to give them to Nue. They were pictures of Rannn and Nue, looking at each other when they didn't think anyone else was watching. Rannn knew that Nue loved them because she was crying and laughing.

Seth of Stars, his wife was too sweet.

Sands and Lita stood up then, but Lita left the private room and then came back with something in her arms. Nue was wide-eyed as Lita came closer and lifted the corner of a little blanket.

Nue gasped. "What is this? Oh my Seth, I'm going to die. Look how cute it is."

Rannn looked in the box and saw a dog-like body and face with a short nose, shimmering purple and white fur, and a long, wispy tail with thorns. The little thing trilled with excitement.

Rannn looked at Sands. "Is that a sheppy from Port Nicca?" Pets weren't allowed on ships or space ports. And Outworld pets were not supposed to be on this side of space at all.

Seeing how his wife was snuggling its face, he needed to stop this before it was too late.

Sands just shrugged. "It was Lita's idea."

"Nue," he said, trying to sound firm.

Her eyes were watering, "He's so cuuuuuuuute. I love him so much."

Good Seth, he was screwed. Rannn noticed how Sands pressed his lips together to keep from smiling.

"Tarq," Rannn whispered.

"Sucker," Sands whispered back.

Nue turned to Rannn with a serious face. "We have to name him. Together."

Yeah, right. "How do you know it's a boy?"

She snorted. "Because he has boy parts. I like the name Carillo."

Rannn thought it sounded horrible.

"You don't like it?"

"I didn't say that."

"Your face did," she said, pressing the sheppy against her neck so she could hold it like a baby.

Sol saved him by stepping forward and giving Nue a Minky pad. "Shady contacted me and told me your Federation ID was released. She was able to force one of the doctors to process your samples. I took the liberty of updating your status and programming a Minky for you."

"Thank you," she said, taking the pad. "And where is Shady so I can thank her?"

"She's still on a flight back."

"Oh."

Several Yunkins who had joined the feast dropped tumaren coins on the table—a traditional wedding gift. Rannn also knew that several of them had already put in their transfer paperwork to follow him to Pegna.

Clalls walked into the galley. He had been absent from dinner, but when he lingered by the door, Rannn wondered what the male had done.

That's when Clalls held out his hand as if he were doing a magic trick. Rannn's lungs stopped with he saw Mother with her shoulder spikes.

He felt a small hand on his shoulder and heard Nue's voice. "That's your mom, isn't it?"

Rannn stood up, pleased to see his mother. But just before he wrapped her in a hug, he saw his sister Adelia and her husband walk in.

His mother sidestepped him and went straight for Nue. "You must be the beautiful bride Clalls told me all about. And he wasn't wrong. Look at you."

Rannn smiled at his wife's blush. He left them to chat and

walked to his sister to give her a hug, despite the way her husband was frowning. "Thank you for coming."

"And miss a chance to see my big brother's chosen wife, I think not."

Rannn snorted. Near the door, Clalls gave a quick salute before he left. A second later, Rannn felt a ping on his Minky pad.

Clalls: *Best gift giver goes to....me. Congratulations, again.*

Rannn: *Indeed. Still retiring? Or are you coming to Pegna? Could use your skills.*

Clalls: *Paperwork is already filed. I know you'll miss me. But a spaceport desperately needs my kind of attention.*

Rannn smiled to himself. He was going to miss that guy.

But not too much.

THAT NIGHT, Rannn sat in bed, his wife slumped over his legs, knocked out because he'd sexed her to sleep. By doing so, he could still hold her as he went through the final part of his day.

Vivra was now the captain of the Garna, and Pax was still commander of Weapons and Tactical Response. He took his time writing Recommendations of Honor for their records.

Clalls put in for retirement and was waiting on acknowledgement. Rannn had signed off on it and wished him luck.

Yon's documents showed that he had resigned and was waiting for approval to relocate to Hetten with Yelena. He'd already purchased a home on the planet and planned to settle there and raise his family. Rannn's finger slid over the screen, drawing his signature to approve the request.

Sasha had resigned too, and had included a note that Sci would be leaving with her. Her document was waiting for acknowledgment. He signed her request and slid his finger to the next crewmember.

Ansel. Rannn skimmed the retirement form and noticed that the Numan had included Orna under the possessions he was taking with him. Nothing else, just his pet. Rannn was about to sign the document when a thought came to him.

Getting out of bed, he gently left Nue on the pillow. He grabbed a pair of pants and slipped into them, not bothering to put on a shirt or shoes. Walking in the dark was no hardship, he knew his cabin by heart. The door was louder than he remembered it being as he opened it, but it didn't wake his wife.

Rannn made his way to the elevator and stopped when he reached the docking bay. As he exited, he saw a figure in the air, floating towards him.

Chollar was also shirtless and without shoes. His bare feet touched the floor and he sucked in a breath as if the metal were cold.

Rannn said, "I want you to do something for me."

Chollar rubbed the back of his head. "Sci's not going to like this."

Rannn didn't care. "Is Sci asleep?"

"Of course. I may have helped him along, but what are brothers for?"

"Good. Because Ansel's a good guy and deserves to be happy. He's not broken. That pet of his proved he can bond. Maybe he can have a family of his own someday."

"I agree."

"So?" Rannn said, hoping that Chollar knew what he was asking. "Will you do it?"

Chollar was silent for several moments, long enough for Rannn to think the Master Elder would say no.

"I'll do it. But it will be slow so neither Sci nor Ansel will notice until it's too late. But I can do it. I can remove his bad memories."

"Thank you."

"You're welcome."

Rannn was quiet for another minute, feeling the emotions that were stronger now than they ever were. "I would like to keep in touch with everyone. Maybe not every year, but every five or so. We can all get together. Your family, Sci's, Yon's, Sands', Pax's, mine, plus Ansel and Clalls."

Chollar smiled a wobbly smile. "You know, growing up on Cerebral, I never would have even considered tolerating someone other than Sci." The male smirked. "But I can say that there isn't anything better than belonging. I've seen what it's done for Sci. He's not the same brother I knew. And yet, he's better now because of you and Sasha and your crew. So, I'll be there. And so will everyone else. I'll make sure of it."

Rannn nodded at the male one last time. "I'll be setting up meetings for Sci as my official Cerebral contact. You can let him know to expect a call."

Chollar grunted. "He'll be delighted."

"Considering that he's the reason we're bridging the sides of space, he'd better be."

BACK IN BED with his wife, Rannn pulled her against his chest and then rested his arms away from her just in case his heart beat too fast. He didn't trust himself to hold her in his sleep, but just like clockwork, she turned, snuggled in, and held him.

While he lay there, he thought about her future. He didn't know if she wanted to get started on their family, or if she wanted to do something else. But there was something he did need from her. Her navigation skills.

There were no defined flight paths for the Outworlds, and he would have to meet with leaders of every planet. Therefore, he would need her to plan his flight. Hell, he needed her with him at all times.

He kissed her shoulder and planned to talk to her about it on the flight to Pegna the next morning.

30

PEGNA

Rannn was in his office on Pegna. It had been a week, and the only people on the space station were the individuals who'd flown with him from the Garna. It was a quiet ship with a skeleton crew.

Not to mention, most of those who'd followed him were from Weapons and Tactical Response.

Not one logistics officer, communications officer, or cook.

Rannn had read at least fifty profiles this morning at his Minky table. The lights from the hologram were starting to hurt his eyes—or maybe it was all the reading.

He was no closer to finding anyone like his last crew. Rannn didn't expect to find exact duplicates, but he had hoped for individuals with specialties.

Sitting to his right, Nue was also reading profiles on his Minky pad.

Rannn had never imagined a relationship where his wife actually worked alongside him. But as soon as she'd woken up, she had offered to help. And he was glad for it.

She'd even brought him breakfast.

His wife was a good thinker.

"Find anyone yet?" he asked.

She pursed her lips and nodded. "Yep."

"Who?"

Nue turned her Minky pad around and said, "Her name is Shady. She says she was with you on Garna, delivered my DNA to Yunkin, gave back my Federation ID and you'd be an idiot if you didn't grant her transfer request because she's already on the station."

Rannn grabbed the pad and read it. He remembered her. The female cyborg who Pax had had trouble with because she was a stickler for the rules. She also got the job done.

Rannn drew his finger across the screen and acknowledged the transfer.

A second later, a knock sounded on his office door. A security protocol measure the previous admiral had installed.

He hit the *allow* button to release the door. A perfectly poised female with brown hair pulled back in a ponytail, and two cybernetic arms stood on the other side.

"Thank you for granting my transfer. I hoped to discuss you letting me take over the logistics of hiring a new crew. I have the time and can screen the profiles faster. I will send you all the employees that match your... expectations."

Nue stood up and walked over with her hand out. "Hi, you're Shady, I assume?"

Shady took Nue's hand and shook it Terran-style.

"Thank you for getting my samples to the lab."

Shady nodded. "Of course, it was my job."

"Thank you for doing a good job." Nue turned around and gave him a small smile, letting him know that Shady was a little...odd.

Just then, the trill of the sheppy sounded from the open

cabin door. Shady stepped in, her cybernetic eyes showing letters scrolling over her irises. Rannn internally cussed because Shady of all beings would raise hell, given she obeyed all rules.

Nue ignored everyone as she cooed at the baby and scooped her up at the door. The little thing had slept with them all night.

When Nue turned around, rubbing her face into the little thing, she said, "Good morning, my little sleepyhead."

Shady was silent for a moment, then did exactly what he'd known she would do. "Pets aren't allowed on ships or stations."

Nue looked at Rannn and then at Shady. Her face fell. "Are you serious?"

Shady spouted off the regulation number and then relayed it verbatim. But when she was finished, she asked, "I have searched my memory, and all Federation archives, and I have no idea what kind of animal that is."

Nue snuggled the pet's face and moved to show Shady Carillo's mug. The little snout stuck out and sniffed the air. "Rannn says it's a sheppy."

Shady tilted her head both ways. "I've never seen a sheppy."

That's when Rannn saw it. The emotional side of the controlled cyborg. So, he asked carefully, "Are you going to enforce this regulation, Shady?"

Shady's eyes snapped to him as if she had been caught doing something naughty. But when he raised a brow and smiled, he added, "Are you?"

Shady looked back at the sheppy and held out her hands. "Can I hold him?"

Nue handed him over. "His name is Carillo."

"Hi, Carillo," Shady said in a baby voice. Rannn watched as the cyborg rubbed her face against the beast's silky-soft fur. "So soft," she added, and then pulled back to look at the pet's face. "I've waived the restriction and now classify you as a service pet. You never have to leave."

Nue looked at him, and he shrugged. Shady was a rule follower, and apparently, a rule bender. He liked that. It reminded him of Yon.

His friend was a rule bender, too. When he wanted to be.

Just then, the Minky table pinged. Orin was calling.

Nue made a gesture with her thumb to the door. "We're going to go."

He nodded and waited for her to leave before he accepted the call. As soon as the video came through, Rannn forced himself not to react. Orin had wide, curled horns protruding from his forehead.

"You didn't take the cure?" Rannn asked.

Orin didn't answer. "How's your mother taking to living in space?"

"She's taking her role as medical mother very seriously. She's already made Arvey give medical screenings to the entire crew."

Orin snorted. "Your crew of seventeen people?"

"Eighteen as of a few minutes ago."

It was silent for a moment, and Rannn took the opportunity to ask, "How's Yunkin recuperating from what happened?"

Orin lowered his head and rubbed the base of his horns. "Rannn, it's madness." When he lifted his head again he said, "The Bolark guards that did as Armsono told them are pissed that they have been detained. They say they were told to do what they did. So many of them have no remorse. And the Yunkins that killed the guards who were tormenting them are also being held until they are seen by an admiral. And that's just the tip of it. Some Yunkins are forcing their family members to take the cure. Others, like myself, prefer to keep the mutations." Orin pointed to his head. "It just..."

"Feels right," Rannn said.

"Yes." Orin looked away for a moment before saying, "My wife and I never had a good marriage, but after this happened, I feel closer to her somehow. Like she and I belong together. Even she decided not to get the cure."

Rannn was pleased to hear that. "Horns look better on you anyway. You're not as ugly."

Orin snorted. "Yeah. But I don't know how you would know that seeing as you obviously went back to being full Yunkin."

Rannn inwardly smiled before lifting his arm and thinking of his wife and all the things he had done to her the other night. Within milliseconds, the spikes emerged, and Orin's eyes widened.

"I didn't get the cure. I just have cooler Night Demon marks than you."

Orin cursed. "Only you, Rannn."

Rannn lowered his arm and got serious. "Do you think the aftermath might lead to a civil war?"

Orin shook his head. "No, but Yunkin is going to go through a rough couple of months as the Bolarks who slaughtered the innocent are punished. And then it will be years before we have equality between the cured Yunkins and the cursed individuals."

"Is that what you're calling yourself? Or is that the label that's going around?"

"It's the term the lawyers have been using in court."

Rannn shook his head. "That label will cause a hard split between the races. Where the cursed are pushed into a lower class. Come up with a better name, for Seth's sake."

"I'm all ears. You have any ideas?"

Rannn scratched his head. Night Kins? Demkins? Day Demons? Yujins…. He kept throwing names around in his head. "Nikings."

Orin's lip curled to the side. "Nikings. I like that. Has a nice ring to it."

"Good. Now spread it wide, and I'll do the same."

Orin nodded and raised his finger like he was about to terminate the call, but he stopped at the last minute and asked, "I heard a rumor about something. Did you get married and not tell me?"

"Yes. To Nue."

Orin's jaw dropped. "The prisoner?"

"She didn't kill anyone, and her lab work proved that." He wouldn't bring up the other charges because those had been wiped clean from the system by someone. Rannn couldn't find the judge who'd sentenced Nue to Debsa, but he would.

"Okay. I didn't know that. But the bigger question is, are you sending her to live on a planet, or are you keeping her on board?"

"She's my wife and mate. She stays with me."

"Doing what? She's not Federation anymore."

"She's still my navigator. Privately hired by me. I also arranged with the council for Nue to map out Federation flight paths through the Outworlds. She's got a lot of space to capture," Rannn said, feeling a little smug that his wife had been hired to do such an important task.

Orin's expression said he knew just how big the job was. "That will take years."

"Probably."

Orin nodded. "Sounds like you have a smart wife."

"I do."

"Congratulations, Rannn. I'm happy for you."

"Thanks. But I'm going to let you go so I can check on her and make sure she hasn't let the sheppy run amuck on the station."

"The what?" Orin said with a frown.

Rannn terminated the call and stood up, pleased that his cousin had chosen to remain a Niking. And also sad that his home planet was going through a rough patch. He hoped it didn't last long, and he prayed to Seth that the turmoil ended quickly.

EPILOGUE

Epilogue – Ten Years Later

Rannn's arms were spiked, and he couldn't calm. Nue couldn't stop giggling. "You haven't been this wired since Seka was born."

Seka, his three-year-old daughter, was a perfect blend of pale skin, purple eyes, and purple and white hair. Rannn couldn't imagine a more beautiful girl in all the universe. She hadn't been born with any Night Demon marks, and Rannn thought they had lucked out.

Until she turned two, and little bones on her arms popped out during a massive tantrum. But instead of all over her arms like his were, his daughter had a single line of black bones that started from her wrist to her elbow.

Seka had hated them at first and cried so hard she fell asleep. In her sleep, they retracted, and his daughter concluded that only sleep could make them go away.

Parenthood had been interesting, to say the least.

Rannn lowered the ramp from the ship and slowly walked to make sure both females in his life were safe. Glancing down at his mate's full, pregnant belly, he realized he couldn't wait to meet his son.

He smiled at the colorful lights, the spinning sparklers, and floating, twinkling lights on the ground. Seka pointed her little finger. "Mom, look."

"I see that. Pretty, huh?"

Rannn spotted Sci standing next to Sasha, who was opening a snack for their daughter. Sci lifted his head in greeting.

Chollar was loading the banquet tables, and Jandy was moving the items around to make it look pretty.

Ansel sat on a chair petting his niskie.

Yon was the closest, and Rannn walked straight to his friend, grabbed his outstretched hand, and pulled him in for a hug. "Long time, Yon."

Yon stepped back after the embrace. "Too long. How's Pegna?"

"There's always something," Rannn answered honestly. Pegna had somehow become a checkpoint for all visitors to pass through. When the Outworlders wanted in, they had to go through Pegna and check in and then undergo a visitation seminar to understand the rules of conduct.

Some were still on the banned list, specifically Boores and Kinglings. Boores because they couldn't communicate properly, and Kinglings because they didn't care about anyone's rules but their own.

"You thinking about retiring?"

"No, I wouldn't know what to do with myself if I did."

Yon nodded. "I know what you mean. After about a year of doing nothing, I started to get really grouchy. So, I applied to the planet Federation. Got a good day job."

Rannn grinned. "Did that stop you from being a grouch?"

"No, but at least I get to take it out on idiots instead of Yelena."

Rannn laughed.

Yon pointed to two Yunkin-looking boys with pitch-black eyes. He said, "Those are my boys, Erannn and Nivo."

It was a Yunkin tradition to name a child after a parent or a person of honor and to put an *E* in front of the name to accent the respect. Rannn pushed down the emotions that surfaced and nodded.

"Are they good boys?"

"Hell no. They're little savages."

Pax walked up with Vivra, drinks in hand, and a big smile. "Hellooooooo," Vivra said, holding up her glass. "Welcome to the party."

"Hello back. How's Garna treating you?"

She slapped the air. "Same as logistics, but instead of managing supplies, I'm managing people."

Chollar and Jandy joined the circle just as three boys whizzed by. They weren't running, they were flying. Rannn knew them well, but by the look on Vivra's face, she didn't. Rannn used a finger to point to the kids. "That's Kava, Gabriel, and Mallik."

Vivra tilted her head. "I'll be honest, I don't know why I never thought about Cerebrals being able to fly."

"We don't do it because it freaks land-walkers out."

Vivra made a face. "I'm not that freaked out. Just surprised."

Sci and Sasha came over. Rannn noticed that Amaree was sitting next to Ansel, petting Orna and talking to the beast. But when the niskie tilted its head, Rannn asked, "Why does it look like your daughter can talk to that animal?"

Sasha harrumphed. "Ansel made a pet translator, and now Amaree constantly wants to talk to every pet, bird, and bug she can find."

Rannn looked at Yon. "No one retires, they just find something else to do."

Sand and Lita arrived ten minutes later with their daughter, Naphtali. Ten minutes after that, Rannn watched the mini-Lita make a slingshot with utensils from the table and use it to fling food at Erannn and Kava.

Kava stood up and pointed at her. "Stop."

She did until he turned around and shot a spoon full of pie at the back of his head. Kava and Erannn ran after her, and Rannn noticed that not one parent looked worried enough to intervene.

Lita looked at Sands. "I bet you ten keleps she tries to sneak onto one of their ships when it's time to leave."

Sands turned as everyone else did as a high-pitched growl rent the air. Kava had Naphtali floating in the air and was turning her around and around. "Twenty keleps she tries to get on Kava's ship."

Gabriel and Mallik ran over, yelling, "My turn to hold her up, my turn."

Jandy touched Chollar's shoulder, but like before, no one did anything.

Seka pushed to leave her mom's arms and walked over to the boys. "Can I fly, too?"

The boys smiled. "You want to fly? You got it."

Nue grabbed Rannn's hands, worried, but she didn't say a word. He squeezed her fingers three times and hoped she understood that everything was all right.

Then, for no reason, Chollar looked up at the sky and stared. Letting his head fall back, he started to laugh.

"What is it?" Rannn asked.

Chollar told the group, "Clalls is coming, and he's got himself a mate."

∼

In bed later that night, Rannn wanted to make love to his wife, but he was dead-tired, and his beautiful female was already turning to snuggle into his side.

The arm spikes had finally receded, and he felt good. Calm. At peace.

Leaning back against the pillow, he tucked a hand behind his head and used his other hand to run his fingers through Nue's hair. It was silky and soft, and he loved the feeling. He kissed her head and wondered what the next reunion would be like.

For so many years, Rannn had thought that he wasn't destined for the simple life. He assumed he'd remain on a ship, captaining a vessel and its crew, dodging dangers and enemies left and right. His old team, his friends—his *family*—had slowly made him realize that there was more to life than just the job. While he loved what he did both then and now, and despite the hardships he experienced, he would never trade his years aboard the Garna and beyond. However, he was happy to finally be able to live. To be. This life he led now, one of admiral, husband, father, was not something he'd expected. But while he was still a captain at heart, now his days were filled with so much more.

And he wouldn't change it for all the worlds or the Outworlds combined.

ACKNOWLEDGMENTS

First, I'd like to thank the Lord for helping me get this book done. Writing is never easy and life always has a way of throwing life emergencies in my face.

Second, I have to thank to beta readers Evon, Jan and Katydid. You three are the best and I appreciate all the time you take to read my early drafts.

Third, I want to thank my editor Chelle Literally Addicted to Detail. She makes my story shine.

Last, but in no way least - I want to thank you, my reader for reading this series and keeping me motivated to keep writing. I get to do what I love because of you. Thank you for the bottom of my heart.

ALSO BY LAYLA STONE

This is the conclusion of the Unexpected Series.

Up next is Clalls's book Unloved Treasures which will kick off the Drifting Treasures series.

As a special bonus I have uploaded the deleted scenes between Captan Rannn and Nue during Unexpected Master. Find out what happened and why Nue hated Rannn so much. Check it out here.

Also, if you fell in love with Clalls during this book, you're not alone. So did I. If you're dying to get inside his mind, read about how he handled the mess of Eldon. Check it out here.

Hang out with me on **Facebook**

To get a notification when a new book comes out check out my **Bookbub**

If you like pictures of sci-fi characters, worlds and spaceships check out on **Instagram**

Join my newsletter if you want to get an inside look to what I'm working on, what's coming out and what I'm planning in the future. **Monthly Newsletter**

BOOK SERIES

Book Series

    Unexpected Series
    Unexpected Hostage
    Unexpected Demon
    Unexpected Commander
    Unexpected Enemy
    Unexpected Master
    Unexpected Captain

Lotus Adaamas Series
    Unintentional Addiction
    Unintentional Obsession
    Unintentional Compulsion – coming 2021

Marnak Series – 90 minute reads
    Uninvited Roommate
    Unstoppable Roommate
    Ungrateful Roommate
    Unannounced Roommate

Untamed Roommate
Unlucky Roommate

Drifting Treasures Series – 90 minute reads
Unloved Treasure